A BAD CASE OF SPRING FEVER

Starlight chewed the bit and tossed his head. Then he began to dance in a little circle. Finally Carole gave up. She rode him to the gate and briskly dismounted. "Starlight, I don't know what's going on with you today, but I think we both need to take a time-out!" Starlight snorted in reply but followed Carole back toward the barn.

"How did it go?" Mrs. Reg asked, looking up from her desk as Carole and Starlight clomped by.

"Oh, okay," said Carole, not bothering to hide the frustration in her voice. "Getting Starlight to behave is just going to take more riding than I thought."

"Well, you know your horse better than anyone," Mrs. Reg said.

Carole buckled Starlight to the cross-ties and removed his saddle and bridle. He fidgeted the whole time, shifting his weight from side to side.

"I hope you get over your spring fever before the Fourth of July, Starlight," Carole said as she quickly brushed the dried sweat from his coat. "Otherwise we'll have to invent a whole new name for whatever it is you've got!"

THE SADDLE CLUB

HORSEFLIES

BONNIE BRYANT

A SKYLARK BOOK
NEW YORK · TORONTO · LONDON · SYDNEY · AUCKLAND

RL 5, 009–012

HORSEFLIES

A Bantam Skylark Book / June 1998

ISBN 0-553-48628-4

Published simultaneously in the United States and Canada.

PRINTED IN THE UNITED STATES OF AMERICA

OPM   0 9 8 7 6 5 4 3 2 1

*I would like to express my special thanks
to Sallie Bissell for her help
in the writing of this book.*

"ARE WE GOING to meet your crazy friends here?" the little boy asked. He held Lisa Atwood's hand tightly as they walked down the lane toward Pine Hollow Stables.

Lisa laughed. "Well, we're going to meet my friends, Jamie. But they're *horse*-crazy. Not *crazy* crazy."

"Oh, I see," Jamie said.

Lisa squeezed Jamie's hand. It was the first day of summer vacation and she'd already gotten a baby-sitting job. She'd promised her parents that she would contribute fifty dollars each month of her own money toward her riding lessons this summer, so she was thrilled when Mrs. Bacon asked her to baby-sit Jamie for the whole week. She needed every penny she could scrape together to continue her lessons, and a weeklong baby-sitting job would go a long way toward her goal.

"Look," Lisa said as they rounded the last curve to the stable. "There they are, waiting for us."

Stevie Lake was sprawled on a hay bale, wearing her usual riding outfit of shirt, jeans, and cowboy boots. Carole Hanson sat next to her in faded breeches and field boots. Lisa blinked and almost stopped. From this distance it looked as if Carole, who was probably the most horse-crazy of the trio, was sitting at the stable reading a book.

"Hi, everybody!" Lisa called. "Sorry I'm late."

"Hi, Lisa." Carole looked up and smiled.

"Who's your friend?" asked Stevie, sitting up.

"This is Jamie Bacon," Lisa said. "Jamie, these are my friends Stevie and Carole."

Jamie smiled, revealing one missing front tooth. "Hi," he said shyly.

Lisa laughed. "These are the other members of The Saddle Club, Jamie. Or at least, most of them." The three girls had started The Saddle Club some time earlier. The only rules were that members had to be crazy about horses, which they were, and they had to help the other members when they got into trouble, which they did.

"I'm going to be baby-sitting Jamie all week," Lisa explained. "And since he wanted to learn something about horses, I thought, What better place to learn than here?"

Carole smiled at the serious-looking little boy. "Have you ever ridden a horse before, Jamie?"

"No," Jamie replied, trying to peek inside the barn. "But it looks pretty neat."

"I asked his mother if it would be okay to bring him to Pine Hollow, and she thought it was a wonderful idea," Lisa said.

"That's great," agreed Carole. "I can't imagine a better place to baby-sit than at a stable."

Lisa spied the paperback book on the hay. "What's this?", she asked Carole, picking it up and peering at the cover. "Greek mythology? Didn't they tell you? School's out. They announced it at assembly last Friday." Lisa was used to her friends' good-natured teasing about her own compulsive study habits. Here was a chance to tease Carole back.

"Can you believe it?" Stevie chimed in. "She's beginning to act just like you! She's actually spending the first day of summer vacation working on a school project that's not even due until fall! I've got so many plans for the summer I won't have time for anything like that." Stevie pulled a piece of straw from her dark blond hair and began to count up all her summer plans. "First, I'm going to ride every day. Then I'm going to swim every day. Then I'm going to dream up a whole bunch of terrific new tricks to play on my brothers. And then I'm going to invent at least fifteen new desserts to eat at TD's." TD's was the ice cream shop where The Saddle Club held many of its meetings. Stevie flopped back on the hay and shook her head incredulously at Carole. "I wouldn't spend a single moment of summer doing schoolwork."

Lisa looked at Carole. "You must admit, Carole, it's not

really like you to spend the first day of summer vacation reading a schoolbook."

"But this isn't just any school project," protested Carole. "This is really cool. Everyone in our class had to choose a summer reading assignment for the new English teacher, and I chose Greek mythology, mostly because Kate Summerfield had already chosen horses. I didn't really want to read about mythology, but when I thumbed through the book, it looked pretty interesting. It's about this wonderful pure-white horse with wings named Pegasus and a beautiful youth named Bellerophon."

" 'Beautiful youth'?" Stevie wrinkled her nose and frowned.

"You know, a handsome young Greek guy—big brown eyes, wavy brown hair, broad shoulders."

"Oh." Stevie nodded. "I get it."

"Anyway, Bellerophon captures Pegasus with a golden bridle that the goddess Athena gave him, and they ride up into the clouds and kill this monster called the Chimera that's got a lion's head and a goat's body and a dragon's tail—"

"Whoa!" Stevie interrupted. "Golden bridles? The goddess Athena? Goat bodies with dragon tails? There goes Carole's summer!"

Carole laughed at Stevie's shocked expression. "That's not all I'm going to do this summer, Stevie. Judy Barker asked me if I'd like to work more hours with her on Tuesdays, to get a better feel for what it's like to be an equine vet. Besides,

I'm going to ride Starlight every day and hang out with you guys."

"Really? You're going with Judy every Tuesday?" Lisa's blue eyes widened.

Carole nodded. "I'm so excited! I'm going to learn a lot."

"That's wonderful. I think your book sounds wonderful, too," said Lisa. "Maybe I'll read it after you finish."

"Actually, it doesn't sound too bad," admitted Stevie. "At least it's about horses."

"But not just any horses," Carole added dreamily. "Horses with wings."

"Do any horses here have wings?" Jamie's high voice broke the silence as each member of The Saddle Club tried to imagine what it might be like to soar through the clouds on a flying horse.

"Sorry, Jamie." Lisa laughed. "I'm afraid not."

"Sometimes it feels like they have wings when they gallop, though," Carole said.

"Or when they go over a double oxer," added Stevie.

Jamie frowned. "Aren't oxers cows?"

This time all the girls laughed. Lisa knelt down in front of Jamie to explain. "Jamie, an oxer's a kind of jump. Would you like to go inside the stable and see what it's like in there? We can give you a tour. In fact, we could even ask Max if he would let you ride one of the ponies."

"Really?" Jamie's eyes shined with excitement.

"We can ask him," replied Lisa.

Stevie jumped off the hay bale. "Let's go! Coming, Carole?" she teased. "Or would you rather stay here and read about Pegasus and the beautiful youth Beetlejuice?"

"Bellerophon, Stevie," Carole said as she shoved the book into her backpack. "And no way. It's time to go see some real horses now."

Lisa took Jamie's hand again, and The Saddle Club began his tour of Pine Hollow Stables. Though the warm summer sunlight sparkled outside, the inside of the U-shaped stable was cool and dark.

Jamie gave a loud sniff and rubbed his nose. "There's something in here that tickles," he said.

"That's hay," explained Carole. "Or maybe sawdust. Smells good, doesn't it?" Carole thought everything inside a barn smelled wonderful—hay, oats, saddles, and especially horses. A gray-and-white cat strutted out from behind a water bucket as they walked toward the stalls.

"That's Seabiscuit," Lisa said as the cat curled himself around Jamie's leg. "He's one of the barn cats."

"Really?" Jamie stroked Seabiscuit's arched back. "How many cats live here?"

"About a thousand," Stevie said.

"Actually, more like ten," Lisa said. "Mice like to nibble at the horse feed, and the cats help get rid of the mice."

As they turned the first corner, Stevie's bay mare, Belle, thrust her head over the stall door and nickered softly in greeting. Carole's horse, Starlight, did the same thing.

"This is my horse, Belle, Jamie," Stevie said as she lifted

Jamie up to give Belle a scratch behind the ears. "She knows my voice. In fact, it's music to her ears."

"And my voice is music to Starlight's ears, Jamie," Carole added. She lifted Jamie up to give Starlight the same kind of scratch.

After Jamie had been properly introduced to Belle and Starlight, Lisa led him down to Prancer's stall.

"Is this one yours?" Jamie asked, scrunching up his eyes as the big Thoroughbred mare leaned over the stall door to sniff his hair.

"No." Lisa sighed wistfully, wishing she would someday have enough money to own a horse. "But she's the one I ride all the time." She smiled as Prancer nuzzled Jamie's ear. "Prancer doesn't like the barn cats, but she loves children."

"She's beautiful," Jamie said, reaching up to stroke Prancer's velvety nose.

"Let's show Jamie the tack room, and then go ask Max if we can take him on a ride," Stevie suggested.

As the four headed to the tack room, various horses stuck their heads out of their stalls, curious to see who was walking by. The group went into a large room filled with saddles, bridles, and all sorts of bits. One wall was dotted with black velvet riding helmets.

"Wow." Jamie stared at all the equipment. "I guess it takes a lot of stuff to ride a horse."

"It sure does." Carole smiled. "You need a saddle so you can sit securely when they gallop."

7

"And a bridle so you can steer them in the direction you want them to go," added Lisa.

"And a helmet so you won't crack your head open when you fall off." Stevie laughed.

"That's right." Max Regnery, their riding instructor and the owner of Pine Hollow, suddenly appeared in the tack room, carrying a clipboard in his hand. "All those things are very important when you ride."

"Max, we were just going to look for you," Lisa said. "This is Jamie Bacon. I'm baby-sitting him, and I was wondering if we could take him for a ride on one of the ponies."

Max looked down at Jamie. Max's normally bright blue eyes looked tired, and lines of fatigue seemed to pull his mouth down. "Have you ever ridden a pony before, Jamie?" he asked.

"No, sir," Jamie replied in a solemn voice.

"I asked his parents for permission to bring him here, Max. They said it was okay," Lisa explained.

Max didn't answer but seemed to stare off at a spot somewhere over Jamie's head.

"Max?" Lisa said. "Are you all right?"

"Uh-huh," Max mumbled through a deep yawn. "Sorry. I'm just not with it today. Maxi's come down with chicken pox and nobody's been able to get any sleep at our house for the last several nights."

"Chicken pox? Oh, Max, we're so sorry!" Carole said with concern. "She's not horribly sick, is she?"

Max shook his head. "Just uncomfortable, mostly. Babies

8

Maxi's age have a hard time scratching, and you know how chicken pox itches. Deborah thinks she must have picked it up here, that morning she stayed in her playpen in my office."

"I don't know," said Stevie. "There's a lot of it going around. My little brother, Michael, spends hours on the phone talking to his friend Shawn Davidson, who came down with it a week ago." Stevie rolled her eyes in exasperation. "Now I can barely get on the phone to make my own calls."

"Which are, of course, all to us." Carole laughed.

"Well, yeah." Stevie shrugged and grinned.

"So, Max, can we give Jamie a ride?" Lisa asked.

Max rubbed his eyes. "Okay. You can give Jamie a ride if you put a helmet on him and promise not to let go of the lead line." He looked at Stevie and Carole. "You two can spot him on either side."

"We promise," said Lisa.

"Then put him on Nickel. He just got back from a beginner class, but he should be okay for a short ride like this."

"Thanks, Max!" Lisa said.

"Have fun." Max yawned again as he returned to his clipboard.

The girls took Jamie down to Nickel's stall. The silver-colored pony looked up from his feed trough when they opened the door. His jaws were still moving and a long wisp of hay dangled from his mouth.

"Uh-oh," Stevie said. "Looks like Nickel was just having a midmorning snack."

"Oh, he won't mind being interrupted." Carole snapped a lead line to his halter. "He'll be done with that mouthful by the time we tack him up. Let's let Lisa and Jamie lead him to the cross-ties while you and I get his tack."

The girls showed Jamie the proper way to lead a horse, and under Lisa's watchful eye, the boy led Nickel to the cross-ties. Carole and Stevie scurried for his saddle and bridle. By the time Nickel was tacked up and ready to go, he had finished his hay.

"Here." Stevie grinned and handed Jamie a riding helmet. "This looks like it might fit."

Jamie put the helmet on and buckled it under his chin. "Wow," he breathed. "Cool!"

"Okay," said Lisa. "Ready?"

They couldn't see Jamie's face, but the black helmet nodded up and down. Together the four of them led Nickel to the stable door.

"Don't forget to touch the horseshoe, Jamie." Stevie pointed to an upright horseshoe nailed to the entrance of the stable. "It's a tradition here at Pine Hollow. Everybody touches it before they ride, and no one has ever gotten seriously hurt."

Stevie lifted Jamie and he touched the horseshoe with one finger; then they led Nickel out into the sunlight. The outdoor ring was empty.

"Okay, Jamie, the first thing to remember is that you always mount a horse from the left side," Carole began.

"How come?"

"Because in the old days, people wore swords attached on their left sides, so they couldn't mount their horses from the right." Of The Saddle Club members, Carole knew the most about horses. "What you do is this. Hold on to the saddle with both hands, put your left foot inside my hands, and I'll boost you onto Nickel. Lisa will hold him like she promised, and Stevie will spot you from the other side."

"Okay." Jamie did as Carole told him, grabbing the saddle and stepping into her intertwined fingers. She gave one heave, and suddenly Jamie was sitting tall in the saddle.

"Wow!" he cried. He turned his head and looked around. "I'm so high up!"

"Put your feet in the stirrups and lightly hold one rein in each hand." Carole helped Jamie adjust his feet and hands. "Horses have sensitive mouths, so you don't want to pull too much on Nickel's bit."

"Okay." Jamie kept his hands just as Carole had placed them.

She grinned up at him. "Ready?"

He nodded.

"Great. Lead on, Lisa."

Slowly Lisa led Nickel and Jamie around the ring, while Carole and Stevie kept pace on either side. Nickel covered the ground with his gentle, swaying walk. Jamie's cheeks

11

grew pink with excitement. "This is fun!" he cried. "Can we go faster?"

Lisa looked over her shoulder at Carole and Stevie. "What do you think?"

"I guess we could trot," said Stevie. "It might be hard to keep up if he canters, though."

"Okay, Jamie," said Lisa. "We're going to do the horse's next fastest gait, which is called a trot. It's a little bumpy, so squeeze tightly with your legs and keep your heels down."

"Okay." Jamie nodded.

Lisa clucked and Nickel moved quickly into a smooth trot, the girls jogging along with him.

"How are you doing up there?" Carole called breathlessly after they had trotted around the ring twice.

"*Grreeaaat!*" Jamie sounded as if he were being bounced on someone's knee.

"Can we stop now?" huffed Stevie. "Before I have a heart attack? Remember, Nickel's got twice as many legs as we do!"

They slowed to a walk, then stopped in front of the gate. "It's time for me to take Jamie home, anyway," said Lisa. "I promised his mother I'd have him back in time for lunch."

"So how did you like riding, Jamie?" Carole asked the beaming child.

"It was great!" he exclaimed. He looked imploringly at Lisa. "Can I come back and ride again sometime?"

She looked up at him. "Maybe we could work something

out with your parents and Max. Right now, though, I need to get you home."

"You and Jamie go ahead, Lisa. Stevie and I can cool and untack Nickel," offered Carole.

"Really?" Lisa asked.

"Yeah, that way you can get back faster and we can take a long trail ride this afternoon," Stevie said with a grin.

"You've got a deal!" said Lisa.

Carole showed Jamie how to dismount. He unsnapped his helmet and handed it to Stevie. "Thanks for the ride," he said softly. "It was lots of fun."

"It was our pleasure, Jamie," replied Stevie. "We of The Saddle Club like nothing better than to introduce people to the fine art of equitation."

"Come on, Stevie," Carole said, pulling Stevie and Nickel toward the stable. "See you later, Lisa. Bye, Jamie. Glad you had a good time. Hope you can come and ride again!"

LATER THAT AFTERNOON, Lisa burst into the tack room. "Hi!" she called. "I figured I might find you two in here."

Stevie and Carole looked up from soaping two bridles.

"Mrs. Reg said this pile of tack needed cleaning," explained Stevie. "So here we are."

All the Pine Hollow riders were expected to help out with stable chores, and Max's mother, Mrs. Reg, who was the stable manager, could usually find plenty for them to do. Though the girls grumbled sometimes, they really didn't mind. The chores always had to do with the health and safety of the horses, and that was important to them.

"It could have been worse," Carole reminded them. "There were a bunch of stalls that needed to be mucked out."

Lisa sat down beside Stevie. "Give me that last bridle and I'll help. That way we can finish faster and get on the trail."

Carole handed Lisa the bridle, and together the girls rubbed the clean-smelling saddle soap into the stiff leather reins.

"Did you get Jamie home in time for his lunch?" Stevie asked as she cleaned green goop off a snaffle bit.

Lisa nodded. "He talked about Nickel all the way back, and his mother gave me a tuna fish sandwich." She smiled. "They're really nice, and Jamie had a wonderful time here at the stable."

"He seems like a neat little kid," said Stevie. "I'm glad you brought him over."

"I wonder what it would be like to have a bridle of gold," Carole said dreamily as she cleaned a noseband. Lisa and Stevie exchanged grins. Carole obviously wasn't paying attention to their conversation.

"Well, you probably wouldn't need to rub it with saddle soap," Stevie said, giggling. "You could just dab metal polish on it, or you could have one of your goddess pals sprinkle it with diamond dust."

The girls looked at each other, then collapsed in laughter.

"What's so funny?" a woman's voice called from the doorway.

The girls turned. Deborah, Max's wife, stood there in jeans and a sweatshirt, a tired smile on her face.

"Oh, just one of Stevie's jokes," replied Lisa. "How's Maxi? Max told us she's got chicken pox."

"She had a terrible night last night. None of us got any sleep. She just itches and itches in places she can't reach to scratch. Babies have such a miserable time with this disease."

"That must be awful," said Carole. "Poor little thing."

"It is awful." Deborah sighed. "The only good thing about it is she'll never have to go through it again. You can only get chicken pox once."

"That's a relief!" exclaimed Lisa.

"Is there anything we can do to help?" Stevie asked.

"I don't think so," Deborah answered wearily. "But thanks for asking. Are you three going on a trail ride?"

"Yes." Carole's dark eyes sparkled. "It's The Saddle Club's first official trail ride of the summer."

"Well, have a good time." Deborah smiled. "I've got to get back to Maxi."

"Bye, Deborah," called Lisa. "Let us know if there's anything we can do to help."

"I will. Thanks." Deborah's voice faded down the hall toward Mrs. Reg's office.

The girls turned back to their job. The once-stiff leather bridles with dirty bits were now clean and hanging along the wall. "These look great!" Carole announced. "I'd say we're done."

"Then let's go," said Stevie. "Last one tacked up is a rotten egg."

Stevie grabbed Belle's lead rope. Carole snagged Starlight's bridle. Lisa scooped up Prancer's currycomb and dandy brush. Then they hurried to their horses' stalls. In a few minutes they all met at the main entrance of the stable, tacked up and ready to go.

"Whew!" said Stevie, out of breath. "I'd call that a draw. Nobody has to be a rotten egg today."

Carole laughed. "Good. I don't feel much like being one after all that bridle cleaning. Which trail do we want to take?"

"Let's do the creek trail," suggested Lisa. "We can have a nice ride across the meadow and then go wading in the creek."

"Sounds good to me," Stevie agreed.

The girls walked their horses to the back of the stable, where the creek trail began, then mounted. Prancer and Belle took off at a trot, eager to go for a run in the woods, but Starlight snorted and balked as if he would rather stay at the barn.

"Come on, boy." Carole squeezed Starlight with her legs as she watched Stevie and Lisa disappear around the first curve. Starlight backed up instead of going forward and twisted his head around to look at Carole. "Everybody's going that way, Starlight!" she cried, squeezing him with her legs again. Finally the bay gelding turned in the right direction and trotted quickly after the other two horses.

Spring fever, Carole thought as Starlight caught up to Prancer. *He's got spring fever and his muscles are tight. I need to ride him a lot more.*

The trail Stevie led them along went a little way through the woods. Above them the sunlight twinkled through a

17

leafy green canopy of trees, and a jaunty mockingbird trilled as they rode past. The sweet smell of blooming honeysuckle drifted through the air. "Isn't this a wonderful day?" Stevie called over her shoulder.

"It's absolutely perfect!" agreed Lisa.

"Want to canter when we get to the meadow?"

"Yes!" Lisa and Carole cried in unison.

They trotted until the woods thinned out into a grassy green meadow speckled with tiny yellow wildflowers. The ground was smooth here and the grass soft. It was the perfect place for a fast ride. The three girls pulled up side by side.

"Everybody ready for the first official canter of the summer?" Stevie asked with a grin.

Carole and Lisa nodded.

"Then let's go, and the last one to the creek's a rotten egg!"

The girls urged their horses into a canter. This time when Prancer and Belle bounded forward, Starlight did not hesitate but ran right along beside them, eager to be first.

Carole shifted her weight over Starlight's withers and relaxed into the horse's gait. She could feel his muscles moving beneath her as his hooves thudded on the grass. The breeze blew cool on her face, and the flower-dotted meadow passed by in a blur. Just ahead was a small tree that had fallen in a storm. As soon as Starlight saw it, he nosed ahead of Belle and Prancer and galloped even faster. To Carole, it seemed as if they were flying. As they approached the tree, Starlight slowed a bit to gather himself; then he jumped high and long over the fallen trunk and branches. Carole closed her eyes as his powerful back legs lifted them into the air, but she wasn't afraid. She suddenly knew exactly what it was like to ride a horse with wings. No wonder Bellerophon loved Pegasus so.

When she opened her eyes, the creek was coming up fast. "Whoa, boy," she said softly, sitting back in the saddle and shortening her reins. Though Starlight settled down into a canter, he tossed his head up and down as if he really didn't want to quit running yet.

"Easy, Starlight," Carole murmured, patting his neck and turning him in a large circle. "You act like you've never galloped before."

Starlight snorted once but finally slowed to a trot, then to a walk. Carole turned to watch as Stevie and Lisa cantered up beside her.

"Gosh, Carole," Stevie said breathlessly. "I only said you'd be a rotten egg. I didn't mean you'd be the rottenest egg on the planet forever!"

Carole frowned. "What do you mean?"

"I mean, you were going fast. Really fast. *Racehorse* fast."

"Oh, Stevie," Carole replied. She knew she'd passed Stevie and Lisa, but she didn't think she'd gone that fast. Stevie tended to exaggerate, anyway.

"No, Stevie's right," said Lisa. "You guys were a blur. I didn't think you were ever going to land after that jump."

Carole couldn't help grinning. "Wasn't that wonderful? I felt just like Bellerophon must have on Pegasus."

Stevie and Lisa exchanged amused glances. "Let's let the

horses graze a little while we go wading," Stevie suggested.
She lifted one eyebrow at Carole. "Unless, of course, there
are some lion-headed monsters around that you and Starlight
want to take on."

Carole laughed. "Not today. Flying on the ground's good
enough for me."

The girls walked their horses to cool them down, then tied
them to some low bushes that grew near the creek. Belle,
Prancer, and Starlight were as much of a club as their riders,
so there was little chance that any of them would run away.
After they had begun to graze contentedly in the deep green
grass, the girls sprawled out on the sun-warmed boulders that
bordered the creek.

"Oh, these boots," Lisa groaned as she pulled off one tall
black boot. "I love them, but they're awfully hot for trail
riding." Lisa's mother insisted that Lisa have just the right
clothes to do all the things she thought proper young ladies
ought to know how to do. She always bought Lisa the very
best, but sometimes Lisa wished her mother would listen to
her more and just buy her what she needed.

"Maybe you'll make enough money baby-sitting Jamie to
buy a pair of short ones," Stevie said as she pulled off her
cowboy boots.

"Jamie's parents would have to go to Europe for six months
for that to happen," Lisa said matter-of-factly. She pulled off
her socks and stuck her feet in the cool water. "Anyway, I've
got to come up with fifty dollars of my own money each
month for riding lessons this summer."

"Ouch." Stevie winced. "That's a lot." She yanked off her socks and plunged her feet into the water. "Ahhh," she murmured. "Bliss."

"He's a nice little boy, though." Carole leaned over the wide, shallow creek and watched as tiny silver minnows darted around their toes. "Baby-sitting him won't be bad. And maybe he can come to the stable again."

Lisa smiled. "It was fun taking him around the ring on Nickel, wasn't it? I felt like, I don't know, a real honest-to-goodness horseback rider."

"I know," agreed Carole. "I did, too. It felt so good to show somebody how wonderful horses and riding are."

Lisa reached down and splashed a handful of cool water where her hair fell against her neck. "I really appreciate your helping me with him today."

"That's what The Saddle Club is for," Stevie chirped. "To help each other out, whenever we need it."

"So you guys really do like Jamie?" asked Lisa.

"Sure," said Stevie. "He's cute. When he grows up, he'll be almost as cute as Phil." Phil Marsten was Stevie's boyfriend. He rode at Cross County Pony Club, and when he and Stevie weren't competing with each other to see who was the better rider, they had wonderful times together.

"Good," Lisa replied. "I'm taking him to the Cross County Fair on Wednesday, and I was hoping you two might want to come along."

Stevie sat up straighter. "I'm already supposed to meet Phil there. But if you and Jamie come along, we can all do the fair

21

together. Can you come too, Carole? Or are you sure you can tear yourself away from Pegasus and Beetlejuice?" There was a mischievous twinkle in her hazel eyes.

"Yeah, Carole," Lisa teased. "I mean, gosh, it's only three months until that project's due. You don't have true Lisa-itis if you're not already thinking about it!"

"You two can laugh," said Carole, "but these stories are really cool." She turned toward Stevie and Lisa and sat cross-legged. "Bellerophon was a prince who had lost his kingdom. King Iobates sent him on a mission to destroy a monster called the Chimera, something no mortal man was supposed to be able to do."

"Is this Chimera Mr. Goat-Breath?" asked Stevie.

"Right. Bellerophon knew he would probably be killed fighting the Chimera, and he was just about to ask for the king's daughter's hand in marriage."

"Gosh," Lisa said softly.

"But he was sworn to do what the king commanded. He was on his way to find the Chimera when suddenly the goddess Athena appeared before him. She gave him a golden bridle and told him to go and put it on Pegasus. That way, on a flying horse, he could kill the monster without being killed himself.

"Bellerophon knew about a spring where Pegasus was supposed to drink, so he went and hid in the bushes and waited. Sure enough, Pegasus came along and Bellerophon jumped on his back. Furious, Pegasus flew high up into the heavens, but Bellerophon hung on and waited for his chance to slip the bridle into Pegasus' mouth. After he did that, Pegasus became as gentle as—"

"Belle!" Stevie interjected.

"No, probably more like Patch," said Carole.

The girls giggled at the thought of Pine Hollow's gentlest, most easygoing horse suddenly sprouting wings and flying off to attack monsters.

Carole continued. "Anyway, after that, Pegasus and Bellerophon flew away to search for the Chimera, and they found it, sleeping at the mouth of a cave. Pegasus dropped down from the sky without a sound, but the Chimera woke up. They had a furious battle that lasted for hours, but in the end Bellerophon chopped off its head. The blood boiled out of its body and turned the ground to ashes."

"So did Bellerophon get back and marry the king's daughter?" Lisa asked.

Carole shrugged her shoulders. "I don't know. I haven't read that far."

Stevie chewed on a blade of grass and stretched out again on the warm rock. "I guess a book like that wouldn't be too bad to read on summer vacation," she admitted.

"I don't think I'll ever mind reading and writing about horses," said Carole.

Stevie grinned at her two friends. "It just seems weird— Carole's reading a book while Lisa's teaching someone about horses!"

Suddenly a high-pitched squeal rang out. The girls turned and looked over at the horses. Starlight had sidled up to Prancer and was trying to bite her ear.

"What on earth?" cried Carole, jumping up and running barefoot over to Starlight. She grabbed his bridle. "He's never tried to do anything like that before."

"Is Prancer okay?" Lisa asked worriedly, hurrying up behind her.

"I think so." Carole felt Prancer's soft ear. There were no scratches, and the skin wasn't broken. "She's okay. I guess Starlight missed." She looked up into Starlight's big brown eyes. "What's the matter with you, Starlight? You've been acting weird all day."

"That is weird for Starlight," agreed Lisa. "He's never been antisocial before."

"Oh, I'm sure it's just spring fever," said Carole, giving Starlight a pat on the neck. "He wouldn't have run that fast through the meadow if he'd been sick. I just need to ride him more and get all the winter kinks worked out of his muscles."

"Well, you'd better work them out soon, or else we'll have to buy Prancer a pierced earring!" Lisa laughed.

"Is everything okay?" Stevie called from her perch on the rocks.

"Just a bad case of spring fever on Starlight's part," Carole called back. "But they're fine."

The horses continued with their grazing, and Lisa and Carole returned to the creek. "Hey, why don't we put our boots back on and ride along the forest trail?" Stevie suggested. "We might see some fawns or fox cubs."

"Fine by me," said Carole. "Starlight obviously needs to work off some excess energy."

Wiggling their toes in the warm sun, the girls let their feet dry, then put their boots back on. They hopped off the rocks and walked over to where their horses were still grazing. Stevie grabbed Belle's bridle and, as usual, was the first to mount up.

"Last one to—"

"Wait, Stevie," said Lisa. "Let's just have a nice, relaxing ride back. We're not in training for the Derby, you know."

"I was just going to say," Stevie replied as Carole and Lisa mounted their horses, "the last one to see something really neat needs glasses."

"Okay." Lisa laughed. "You're on."

For the rest of the afternoon, the girls rode over the rolling Virginia countryside, splashing through streams and cantering across the broad, open meadows. Stevie found a nest of newly hatched killdeers, and Lisa had to calm Prancer down when a graceful, honey-colored doe burst from the woods and bounded across the path right in front of them.

"That's one for me and one for Lisa," Stevie said as they trotted three abreast at a wide place in the trail. "Haven't you seen anything neat, Carole?"

"I've seen lots of neat things," said Carole. "You two just see them first." Actually, Carole had been looking more at

Starlight than at the plants and animals on the trail. Riding all afternoon hadn't done him the good she thought it would. Usually he was a cooperative, dependable horse. Since they'd left the creek, he'd shied at a leaf falling from a maple tree, he'd refused to go over a tiny mud puddle, and he'd tried again to bite Prancer, this time on the rump. It was as if he was determined to see how naughty he could be.

"You'll do better tomorrow, boy," Carole whispered. Starlight tossed his head and tried to go around Belle on the right, but Carole sat up straighter in the saddle. "I know just what you need, Starlight. A good ride every day this summer." She smiled down at her horse. *It's a good thing you've got me to take care of you,* she thought. *I know just what to do.*

3

The great white stallion broke into a gallop. . . . Faster and faster he went; then suddenly he spread his wings, and with one massive downstroke they lifted him straight up into the air. Higher than any eagle, more swiftly than a falcon he flew, his graceful white neck arched and gleaming in the sun . . .

A CAR HORN BLASTED. Carole jumped. The paperback fell out of her hands and she looked up, blinking in the bright sunlight. Just a moment ago she had been in ancient Greece, soaring through the clouds on Pegasus. Now she had suddenly plummeted back to Willow Creek, Virginia, where she sat in front of Pine Hollow Stables, waiting for Judy Barker to pick her up.

"Hi, Judy!" she called to the figure waving from the familiar blue pickup. Quickly Carole gathered up her book and the brown-bag lunch she'd packed and hurried out to the truck. Judy watched her and smiled.

"Hi," Judy said as Carole climbed in beside her. "I'm sorry if I startled you. You looked like you were thousands of miles away."

"Oh, not really." Carole felt a tinge of embarrassment warm her cheeks. "More like thousands of years." For weeks she'd been excited about spending Tuesdays with Judy, and here she was, on her very first trip, daydreaming about Pegasus. "I was just catching up on my reading while I waited. It's about this horse with wings."

Judy smiled. "You mean Pegasus?"

Carole looked over at her in astonishment. "You know about Pegasus?"

"Oh, yes," said Judy, checking her rearview mirror. "He was my all-time favorite character in Greek mythology."

"Wasn't it wonderful what he and Bellerophon did?" Carole was thrilled to find somebody else who knew about this fabulous horse and rider.

"It was super. When I was little I used to wish I could grow up and find a whole island of winged horses, just like Pegasus. Then I could ride and fly anywhere I wanted to." Judy chuckled as she eased the truck out into the street. "Now I guess I'd have to find one with a trailer hitch so that I could carry all my medical supplies along, too."

28

Carole laughed at the idea of Judy's making veterinary calls on a winged horse that pulled a trailer. She settled back in the seat and stashed her lunch under it.

"So where are we going today?" Carole asked as they turned right onto a four-lane highway.

"Out to a new client. Mr. and Mrs. Albergini at Shady Lane Farm. They moved here recently from southern California."

"What kind of horses do they have?" Carole pictured the Alberginis bringing some exotic stock of Bashkirs or Friesians to Virginia.

"I'm not sure," Judy replied. "They called me a week ago to set up a general vet check. This should be an interesting call for you to help with, just because it is routine."

Carole looked out the window as Judy drove down the highway. Tuesday was as perfect a day as Monday had been, with sunshine and high white clouds floating across the sky. She gazed out the window as they cruised through the countryside. If she squinted a certain way at one cloud, she could just imagine a single rider on a winged horse soaring high above them.

They drove for several miles until they came to a bright blue mailbox with the words SHADY LANE in silver letters. Judy turned down the gravel driveway, which twisted through a grove of tall oak trees. "Guess this is why they named it Shady Lane," she said as the truck bounced over a rut in the tree-covered road.

The driveway ended at a large riding ring filled with brightly painted jumps. To the right was a long barn, where an older man and woman stood waiting.

"Hi," Judy said as she pulled up in front of the couple. "Mr. and Mrs. Albergini?"

"That's us." The man wore a golf shirt, jeans, and jodhpur boots. "I'm Sam and this is my wife, Claudia."

Mrs. Albergini wore glasses with purple frames and a brightly colored Hawaiian dress. She smiled at Carole and Judy. Carole smiled back. By their outfits, Carole figured that Mr. Albergini must be involved with the horses, while maybe Mrs. Albergini gave hula lessons on the side.

Judy got out of the truck and introduced herself to the couple. "I'm Judy Barker, and this is my assistant, Carole Hanson," she said as Carole got out of the truck and stood beside her.

"Pleased to meet you." Mr. Albergini shook Judy's hand firmly. He had a tiny mustache and brown eyes that crinkled up when he talked. "We've heard that you're the best vet in the county."

"Yes," Mrs. Albergini chimed in. "We feel very lucky to have you stop by."

"Thanks," said Judy. "I appreciate the compliment. Is there a particular horse you're having problems with?"

"Well, most everything is fine." Mr. Albergini ran his hand through his thinning gray hair. "But I've got three that have been acting a little squirrelly lately. I can't figure out what could be the matter."

Judy gave the Alberginis a reassuring smile. "Let's go have a look at them and see how we can help." She turned to Carole. "Would you bring my bag and lab kit from the truck?"

"Right away." Carole felt a thrill of excitement as the Alberginis watched her get Judy's equipment. It was almost as if she were a real vet herself.

"Would you two doctors like some cookies and lemonade?" Mrs. Albergini called as Judy and Carole began to follow Mr. Albergini into the barn.

"No thanks," Judy replied with a smile.

"Well, I'll be in the house if you need me," Mrs. Albergini called.

"Does your property have a lot of standing water, Mr. Albergini?" Judy asked as they jumped over a murky brown puddle.

"Only around the barn. The rest of the land drains well. We have a creek that runs along the back."

"I see."

Carole noticed a frown on Judy's face; she realized that Judy had already begun diagnosing the situation when she'd only asked about a mud puddle. What did a mud puddle have to do with horses being sick?

The Alberginis' barn was a long structure with five stalls on either side. Though the ventilation was good, the air was thick with gnats and flies.

"Where do you spread your manure, Mr. Albergini?" Judy asked, slapping a deerfly that had landed on her arm.

31

"Just right out there in back of the barn." Mr. Albergini slapped a mosquito off his own arm. "But it's fenced so that the horses can't get into it."

"I see." Judy smiled. "Now, where are the horses you've been having problems with?"

"Two are over here." Mr. Albergini led them to the far two stalls on the left side of the barn. In the first was a beautiful chestnut mare. She lifted her head and nickered when Judy and Carole came close. Her eyes were deep brown and very kind.

"This is Lady Jane," Mr. Albergini said, giving the horse a pat on the neck. "She's won lots of barrel-racing competitions, and we'd like to breed her, but I can't get her to eat anything."

"How long has she been like this?" asked Judy, a frown once again wrinkling her forehead.

"Oh, about a week. She's such a sweet, good horse. I'm beginning to think something might be wrong with her."

"Carole, would you hold her?" Judy asked.

Carole got the lead line that hung next to Lady Jane's stall, snapped it to her halter, and led her out in front of Judy. Lady Jane sighed once and stood quietly, almost resting her head on Carole's shoulder. "Good girl," Carole whispered, rubbing her soft nose.

Judy examined Lady Jane's mouth, eyes, ears, and feet. Then she rummaged in her bag for her stethoscope and listened to her heart and lungs. She felt down each of the mare's legs, then along her spine.

32

"I'm not palpating anything abnormal," Judy reported to Carole. Judy ran her hands along Lady Jane's muscular shoulders and thighs. She felt behind the mare's back legs and under her tail. "Everything seems okay," she said. "She's a good strong quarter horse, and she looks like she would throw nice foals."

She gave Lady Jane a pat on the withers. "Let's check her for worms. A worm infestation would certainly put her off her feed."

"That's a good idea, Dr. Barker," said Mr. Albergini. "None of these horses have been wormed since last fall."

"Okay." Judy turned to Carole. "Remember that we need to do a worm check on all the horses."

"Will she start eating again if we get rid of her worms?" Carole asked.

"She should," Judy said. She gave the mare a scratch behind her ears. "She seems to be a sound horse otherwise. I'll do some blood work on her later to make sure there aren't any other problems, but after a cleanup and a tube worming, she should start eating again and make a wonderful mother."

"That's good news," Mr. Albergini said as Carole walked the mare back to her stall.

"Who's next?" asked Judy.

"Next is Joker." Mr. Albergini walked to the next stall, where a shaggy gray Shetland pony stood munching hay. There was an impish look about him, as if he might enjoy romping in some goofy gymkhana race with balloons at-

33

tached to his head. For some reason, Carole thought of Stevie.

"Does Joker have any special problems?" Judy asked as Carole led the pony out of the stall. Joker seemed frisky and eager to leave the confines of the stable.

"Calm down, boy," Carole said with a laugh as the little horse stomped one foot and twitched his tail.

"He's a great little guy, although he has begun acting up lately. He threw my granddaughter off the other day."

"Goodness. Was she hurt?" Judy asked.

"Only her pride." Mr. Albergini laughed. "Still, I hope Joker's not becoming an unsafe mount."

"Well, let's see." Judy performed the same examination of Joker that she'd done of Lady Jane. Joker shifted and wiggled and fidgeted the whole time.

"Find anything wrong?" Mr. Albergini asked as Judy ruffled her hands through Joker's shaggy coat.

"It's hard to tell through all this hair," Judy said. She folded her arms and stepped back from Joker; then she reached into her medical bag and took out a notepad. "Let's try something," she said. "Carole, I want you to hold this pad under Joker's chin."

"Sure." Carole stepped forward and held the notepad.

"Okay," said Judy. "Let's see what we get here." She held up Joker's head and scraped her fingernails along the underside of his jaw. All sorts of dirt and dandruffy material fell onto the white paper. Judy examined it closely. "Look at this," she said to Carole and Mr. Albergini. They bent over the pad and looked. A number of tiny, brown, cigar-shaped bugs squirmed on the paper.

"Gross." Carole scrunched up her nose. "What are they?"

"Lice," Judy replied. "Joker's got a bad case of lice. Lice make horses miserable. They itch all the time and can't scratch properly and it wears them out." She looked at Mr. Albergini. "That's what's making Joker cranky."

"I'll be darned," Mr. Albergini said, amazed.

"I think Joker needs a summer haircut, a good bath with some lice shampoo, and insecticide spray." Judy gave Joker a pat on his rump. "He'll be fine. Before we leave I'll do some blood work on him, too, just to be sure that's the only thing wrong."

Mr. Albergini and Judy moved to the next horse while Carole put Joker back in his stall. The little horse lowered his head sadly when he was put up again. "Don't worry," Carole said, giving his mane a quick rub. "You'll be playing in the meadow with your buddies in no time."

They worked their way down that side of the barn. The next three horses were fine, only needing a routine worming. Then they crossed to the other side of the barn.

"Who have we got over here?" Judy asked, swatting at a fly that buzzed around her right ear.

"This is Spirit." Mr. Albergini got the lead line and led Spirit out himself. She was a delicately formed black Arab mare with a small white star on her forehead. Though she had a pretty, fine-boned face, her coat was dull and there was a hopeless look about her eyes. "She just hasn't been herself.

Acting up when she's ridden, spooking at familiar things. Just acting nutty in general."

"Hi, girl," Judy said softly as she examined Spirit. Carole watched Judy's frown grow as she felt Spirit's legs and along her belly. "I know exactly what's the matter with this horse."

"What?" Carole and Mr. Albergini said in unison.

"Both of you, lean down here and feel these bumps."

Carole and Mr. Albergini did as Judy asked. Carole felt a whole line of swollen blisters the size of quarters. When they touched them, Spirit jumped as if she'd been pinched. "What are they, Judy?" Carole asked.

"Spirit is allergic to mosquito bites," Judy said. "They've bitten her all along her girth line." She looked down at Mr. Albergini. "Was Spirit ridden near those puddles of water?"

Mr. Albergini nodded. "That's where my son last rode her."

"Then that's where she picked up those bites." Judy patted the pretty little horse. "I can give her some medicine for the bites. But let's try to make sure this doesn't happen again."

Mr. Albergini put Spirit back into her stall. Judy and Carole worked their way down the rest of the barn. Other than one gelding needing to have his teeth floated, all the rest of the horses were fine. When they had finished with the examinations and had taken all the blood samples, Carole's shoulders ached with fatigue, but Judy had just started. She sat down on a bale of hay and began to talk.

"Mr. Albergini, have you been in the horse business long?" she asked, again swiping at the pesky flies that swarmed around her face.

Mr. Albergini's eyes crinkled up. "No. My wife and I moved here from San Diego to be near our son, who works in Washington. We bought this farm lock, stock, and barrel two months ago so that our grandchildren could ride. We rode horses in California, and we've read a lot about keeping horses since we've been here, but we're certainly not experts."

Judy gave him an understanding smile. "Well, there's nothing wrong with not being horse experts as long as you're willing to keep learning. Your stable is in basically good shape, but you need to work harder at keeping things clean."

"Oh?" Mr. Albergini said.

"Yes." Judy took a pen from her shirt pocket and began writing on the notepad. "First, you need to get rid of those puddles of water. Unlike southern California, we get a lot of rain in Virginia. Standing water attracts mosquitoes. Mosquitoes carry all sorts of serious equine diseases, and you've already got one horse that's highly allergic to them."

Mr. Albergini frowned. "I honestly hadn't thought of that."

Judy continued. "Next, you need to start carrying the manure a lot farther away from the barn and spreading it over the ground so that the sunlight can kill the bacteria and organisms in it. Flies breed in piles of manure, and flies are a major irritant to both horses and riders."

Mr. Albergini chuckled. "We have fifty acres. I'm sure we could find another place to put it."

"Third, you need to scour this entire barn with insecticide and set up a program to spray for flies and ticks. You'll need to spray your horses, too, and be extra protective of those that are really sensitive, like Spirit. I can tell you what special products to buy and how to use them."

"That would be wonderful, Dr. Barker."

Carole watched as Judy scribbled more notes on her pad. Though a few of Mr. Albergini's horses had suffered because of his ignorance, she felt sorry for him. She could see how bad he felt.

Suddenly Mrs. Albergini appeared in the doorway. She carried a tray with three tall glasses of lemonade and a plate of cookies.

"I know you said you didn't want any lemonade, but you've been out here so long I know you must be hungry and thirsty." She blinked at Judy and Carole. "Please don't tell me any of our horses are seriously ill!"

"No, Mrs. Albergini, not at all," Judy reassured her quickly. "Most of your horses are in good shape. Your barn just has some basic sanitation problems that need to be taken care of."

"Really?" Mrs. Albergini calmed down as she handed her husband the tray and gave Judy and Carole their lemonades. "So it's something we can fix?"

"Oh, yes," replied Judy. "But I recommend that you hire a

professional trainer for a while, at least until you learn more about basic horse care."

"Why, what a good idea!" Mrs. Albergini beamed as she passed around the plate of cookies.

Carole took the glass and cookies Mrs. Albergini offered. The cold lemonade tasted good after working in the hot, fly-infested barn, and the chocolate chip cookie was still warm and gooey from the oven.

"Okay, Mr. and Mrs. Albergini," Judy said as she handed them several sheets of notepaper. "Here are my written instructions. Carole and I will take our blood samples back to the lab and get you the results of our tests in about a week. Beyond that, I have just one other request."

"What's that?" Mr. Albergini's eyebrows raised in alarm.

Judy grinned. "Would you enclose your chocolate chip cookie recipe when you pay my bill? These are the best cookies I've ever tasted!"

THE ALBERGINIS WAVED as Judy and Carole pulled away from Shady Lane Farm. Carole waved back, then turned around in her seat and faced Judy. "They were nice, weren't they?"

Judy smiled. "Yes, very nice. They just need to work on their barnkeeping a little better."

"Do you think they'll do all the things you recommended?" Carole was worried that the Alberginis might get confused by everything Judy had told them.

"I'm going to keep an eye on them. I gave them the names

of two good trainers and a barn helper. After a month or so with them, they should be on the right track." Judy grinned at Carole as the truck bounced along the bumpy driveway. "So, how did you like your first morning as a vet's assistant this summer?"

Carole thought of the sweet mare Lady Jane and cute little Joker and pretty Spirit. "It was terrific," she replied softly. Though her head spun from all the procedures they had done during the day, she felt wonderful when she realized that, in a small way, she had helped some sick horses feel better.

"I haven't worn you to a frazzle, have I?" Judy asked.

"Oh, no," Carole assured her. *This is going to be a great summer*, she thought as she watched another white cloud that looked like Pegasus. *I'm learning all about horseflies and all about flying horses—and what could possibly be better than that?*

"Bye!" Carole called as Judy pulled away from Pine Hollow. "See you next Tuesday!"

Judy waved back, and Carole turned and walked toward the stable. *How wonderful,* she thought as the afternoon sun beamed down on her shoulders. *The whole day spent learning about horses!*

She looked at Pine Hollow nestled among the trees. How different it was from the Alberginis' stable. Max took such good care of everything. He filled the ditches and low places around the stable with gravel so that rainwater wouldn't collect in them. Red O'Malley trucked the manure to a field far away from the horses. Then, after it had baked in the sun for a whole year, he bagged it and gave it to the neighboring gardeners for compost. Inside the building itself, brand-new

41

electric bug zappers killed any flies and mosquitoes that survived the monthly insecticide spraying program. Carol smiled to herself as she walked into the cool dimness of the stable. You probably couldn't find a single fly within five miles of Pine Hollow!

"Well, hi, Carole." Mrs. Reg looked up from her desk as Carole passed by. "I didn't expect to see you here this early. I thought you were out on rounds with Judy."

"I was," replied Carole. "We did one whole barn full of horses, and then Judy had to take the blood samples back to the lab."

Mrs. Reg smiled. "Did you learn a lot?"

"Tons," said Carole. "Now I've got to go give Starlight a good workout. I promised him I'd ride him every day and help him get rid of his winter kinks."

Mrs. Reg looked at her quizzically. "Winter kinks? This time of the year?"

"Oh, yes," Carole assured her. "Starlight's got spring fever. He hasn't been ridden nearly enough."

"Well, you sound as if you know what's best." Mrs. Reg returned her attention to the paperwork on her desk.

Carole thought about Starlight as she walked toward his stall. It did seem odd that he was still acting as if he had spring fever, particularly since she'd ridden him a lot during the school year. Even so, she hadn't ridden him every day, and Starlight was an athletic, energetic horse. *He just needs a lot more exercise,* she told herself, *and this is his way of telling me.*

"Hey, boy," she called softly when she reached his stall.

Starlight stood with his rear end to the door. He turned and flicked one ear at Carole when she greeted him, but he did not answer her with his usual friendly nicker.

"What's the matter, Starlight?" Carole asked. "You look like you're mad at me."

Starlight blinked once, then turned to face Carole. He allowed her to rub his nose, but he did not seem particularly glad to see her.

"Are you jealous because I spent my morning with other horses?" Carole asked, brushing Starlight's bangs away from his eyes.

The big gelding snorted. Carole rubbed his nose some more, then clipped a lead line to his halter and led him out of his stall. "I'll groom you fast," she said as she snapped him to some cross-ties. "Then we can get out of the stable fast and have a nice ride."

In a few minutes she had Starlight tacked up and ready to go. He followed her willingly out of the stable, but then, as she was about to lead him into the outdoor ring, he stopped and balked, just as he had before the previous day's trail ride.

"Starlight!" Carole cried in surprise. "Not this again. What is the matter with you?"

Starlight stood with his ears back, staring at the cavalletti exercise Max had set up. Cavalletti were long, skinny poles that were put across a horse's path to help even out their strides. The goal was to ride through the cavalletti without the horse's hooves touching any of them along the way.

"Those are just cavalletti in the ring. You've trotted over them a million times before!" Carole gave Starlight a pat on the neck. He shook his head but allowed her to lead him into the ring.

Carole closed the gate behind them. An intermediate riding class had just ended, so she and Starlight had the ring to themselves. "Maybe some cavalletti work would be a good idea," she said, leading Starlight over to one side of the ring. "It might help you get more into the swing of things."

She pulled down the stirrup irons, gathered the reins, and climbed into the saddle. When she put her weight fully on his back, Starlight gave a little jump and tried to move sideways.

"Whoa, boy," she said quietly, turning him in a wide circle and letting him get used to her being on his back. He snorted again and jerked his head up and down.

Carole urged him into a walk, ignoring the cavalletti for the moment. Starlight fidgeted with his bit, then finally settled down. "Good boy," Carole praised him as they rounded a turn. "That's the Starlight I know and love."

They did two circles of the ring at a walk, then a trot.

"Let's try walking the cavalletti now," Carole said, reining Starlight over to where the course began. Starlight looked at the half dozen poles stretched out on the ground before him and came to a dead stop.

"Come on, Starlight," Carole insisted, pressing with her legs and sitting forward in the saddle. Again Starlight

44

chewed his bit, but he began to move forward over the cavalletti.

Thunk! Starlight's far rear hoof hit one cavalletti, then one
of his front hooves hit another. Carole almost dropped her
reins in shock. Starlight had done this exercise perfectly for
years, and now he was acting like a green colt!

She rode to the top of the course again and urged Starlight
into a trot. This time he didn't chomp his bit, but he swished
his tail as if he were mad. He began a stiff, up-and-down trot
and thunked three out of the six cavalletti.

"Whoa." Carole reined him up in the center of the ring.
She unbuckled her helmet and wiped the sweat from her
forehead. She frowned, wondering why Starlight was having
so much difficulty with such an easy exercise. Then she remembered how much better he had behaved the day before
after his run in the meadow.

"I know what we'll do," she said, dismounting and leading
him toward the gate. "We'll go for a good canter in the back
paddock and see if that doesn't work off some of your excess
energy." Starlight nickered, seeming to agree.

Carole walked him to the back paddock and remounted.
Starlight seemed more like his old cooperative self this time.
He moved easily from a walk to a trot when Carole asked
him; then, when she nudged him behind his girth for a
canter, he took off like a rocket.

"You like that, huh?" Carole asked as Starlight made a
flying lead change. For the first time that afternoon, she relaxed. She felt as if she had her old horse back. She sat a

little more forward in the saddle and pressed Starlight into a gallop. Suddenly the fence posts began to fly by. Starlight's hooves thundered on the ground just like the horses in Western movies. His mane tickled her nose as she crouched over his shoulders, and again she wondered what it must have been like when Pegasus flew. Did Bellerophon have to hang on tight? Or were Pegasus' wings so strong and smooth that all Bellerophon had to do was relax and watch the earth passing far below him?

They were going so fast, Carole thought that if Starlight had magically sprouted wings like Pegasus, it would have taken one swooping stroke for them to be high in the air, soaring like hawks over Pine Hollow and the hills beyond.

They galloped around the huge paddock until Carole was out of breath and Starlight had white flecks of sweat on his withers. She slowed him to a canter, then to a relaxed trot.

"Did that feel good, boy?" Carole patted his damp neck. She knew she would have to ride him at a walk forever to cool him down, but it had been worth it. She had known all along that lots of galloping was the cure for what ailed Starlight. It worked every time.

When Starlight had finally cooled off, Carole led him out of the paddock and back to the riding ring. "Let's try those cavalletti again, Starlight," she said. "I know you can do better than the last time."

Just as before, they circled the ring at a trot without going over the cavalletti; then Carole guided Starlight over the first pole. Again she heard the now familiar *thunk* of his rear hoof

46

hitting the pole. *Okay,* she thought, *maybe he's just off stride a little.* Then *thunk, thunk, thunk.* Starlight hit every cavalletti with his rear hoof. She reined him in again. "Oh, Starlight!" she cried. "You're getting worse instead of better!"

Starlight chewed the bit and tossed his head. Then he began to dance in a little circle. Finally Carole gave up. She rode him to the gate and briskly dismounted. "Starlight, I don't know what's going on with you today, but I think we both need to take a time-out!" she said as she led the horse back toward the stable. Starlight snorted in return but followed Carole obediently.

"How did it go?" Mrs. Reg asked, looking up from her desk as Carole and Starlight clomped by.

"Oh, okay," said Carole, not bothering to hide the frustration in her voice. "Getting Starlight to behave is just going to take more riding than I thought."

"Well, you know your horse better than anyone," Mrs. Reg said.

CAROLE BUCKLED STARLIGHT TO the cross-ties and removed his saddle and bridle. He fidgeted the whole time, shifting his weight from side to side.

"I hope you get over your spring fever before the Fourth of July, Starlight," Carole said as she quickly brushed the dried sweat from his coat. "Otherwise we'll have to invent a whole new name for whatever it is you've got!"

47

5

"LOOK! THERE'S CAROLE!" Jamie Bacon's voice rang out from the backseat of Mrs. Atwood's car. "But where's Stevie? Isn't she supposed to come with us?"

"Yes, Jamie, she is," Lisa reassured the excited little boy as they pulled up to Pine Hollow. "She might be visiting her horse, or she might not be here yet."

"Then can we go see Nickel?" Jamie unbuckled his seat belt and pressed himself against the front seat, where Lisa and her mother sat.

"Maybe." Lisa rolled down her window and waved at Carol.

"Oh, please?" Jamie began to jump in the backseat. "Please?"

"Jamie, honey, calm down," Mrs. Atwood said gently.

48

"You don't want to tire yourself out before you even get to the fair." She parked the car and turned to Lisa. "I'll wait here in the parking lot. Why don't you take Jamie up to visit the pony for a minute? Maybe Carole knows where Stevie is."

"Okay." Lisa opened her door. "Come on, Jamie."

Jamie bounded out of the car and ran toward the stable. "Hi, Carole!" he called. "We're going to the fair! Will you ride the merry-go-round with me? Where's Stevie? Can we go see Nickel?"

"Gosh, Jamie." Carole laughed. "You sound a little excited. Yes, I'll ride the merry-go-round with you."

"Hi, Carole." Lisa hurried up, already out of breath from chasing after Jamie. "Where's Stevie?"

"She just called the stable and left Mrs. Reg an emergency message for us," Carole reported. "She said not to leave without her, that Chad had put crunchy peanut butter in her best sneakers and she had to clean them out before she could come, but she would be here in ten minutes."

"Uh-oh," Lisa said with a grin. "I know an older brother who's gonna get revenged."

Carole laughed. "This one should really be good. I already feel sorry for Chad."

"So can we go see Nickel?" Jamie pulled Lisa by the arm.

"Well . . . ," Lisa began.

Suddenly there was a shrill whistle from the parking lot. "Hey, everybody!" a voice called. "Aren't we going to the fair?"

They all turned. Stevie stood by the Atwoods' car, waving. The Lakes' station wagon was disappearing around the curve. Mrs. Lake must have taken mercy on Stevie and dropped her off.

"I guess you'll have to visit Nickel some other time, Jamie," Lisa said. "Stevie's here and we need to go."

"Aw." Jamie stuck out his lower lip. "I want to see Nickel."

"Well, how about if the first thing we ride at the fair is the merry-go-round?" suggested Lisa. "You've been talking about it all morning, so we'll do that as soon as we get there."

"Okay." Jamie brightened and skipped back to the car.

Lisa looked at Carole proudly. "I think we created a brand-new horseman the other day."

"I know." Carole beamed. "Isn't it terrific?"

They piled into Mrs. Atwood's car, where, all the way to the fair, Stevie complained about her brother.

"I can't believe Chad would do something that nasty," Stevie fumed. "He knew this was important. He knew I was going to see Phil today."

"I thought you two had declared a truce," said Carole.

"I thought so, too. But Chad re-declared war when he stuffed all that goopy peanut butter in my shoes. It took me forever to get it out!" Stevie sat back and crossed her arms. "Just wait. I'll think of a trick to play on him that will go down in the history books."

"How much longer till we get to the fair?" Jamie asked

50

Lisa. Though he had listened politely to Stevie's ranting and raving, Lisa could tell that he could hardly wait to get to the fair.

"We're almost there," Mrs. Atwood called from the driver's seat. She turned off the highway down a dusty, unpaved road. Just across a large field they could see a tall Ferris wheel, a ride that looked like a giant pirate ship, and a set of enormous swings.

Mrs. Atwood dropped them off at the gate, reminding them that she would pick them up at three. "Don't ride anything that will make you queasy," she called as they got out of the car. "Remember, Lisa, you've got a sensitive stomach!"

"Bye, Mom," Lisa said wearily as her mother drove away.

"Come on!" Jamie grabbed her by the hand and pulled her toward the front gate. "Let's go ride the merry-go-round!"

They had just paid their admission fee when they heard a familiar voice behind them. "Why, there's The Saddle Club. Fancy meeting them here!"

The girls turned. Phil Marsten, Stevie's boyfriend, stood there smiling. He wore jeans and a green polo shirt and a space helmet made out of bright pink foam. "Pretty cool hat, huh?" He laughed, nodding and making the two sparkly antennas wiggle. "I won it at the bottle toss."

"Sorry we're late, Phil," Stevie called. "I had a rather sticky encounter with my brother."

"No problem," said Phil. "The fair will be here all day

long." He looked down at Jamie and gave him a warm smile. "Is this Jamie, the famous horseman?"

"Yes," Lisa said. "And he really wants to ride the merry-go-round."

"Well, let's go." Phil pointed past the fortune-telling booth. "I think I saw it right over there."

Jamie pulled Carole and Lisa toward the merry-go-round. Stevie and Phil followed, laughing together. It was a beautiful day for a fair—bright and sunny, with the sound of music drifting on a gentle breeze. A gypsy with silver earrings called to them to have their fortunes told. A local high-school band was trying to sink its director in a dunking booth. The director made faces and called funny insults to his students while they tried to hit a target with a softball and plunge him into a tank of water. Everyone was laughing and enjoying the spectacle when suddenly Jamie stopped.

"Oh no!" he cried, tears edging his voice. "Look!"

Everyone looked where he pointed. The merry-go-round was still and dark. All the horses were frozen in place, and not one note of cheerful music filled the air. A yellow plastic band had been tied around the ride with OUT OF ORDER printed in thick black letters.

Jamie looked up at Lisa and Carole and Stevie, his lower lip quivering. "Is it broken?"

Lisa bent down and gave him a hug. "That's what the sign says, Jamie. But there are lots of other rides here that are just as much fun as the merry-go-round."

"Do they have horses?"

"Well, no, but—"

"I want to ride on the merry-go-round!" Jamie crossed his arms and stamped his foot.

"Hey, come on, Jamie." Phil knelt down beside him. "There are lots of neat rides here. There's the Tilt-A-Whirl carousel and the Typhoon and the Spyder and a really cool Ferris wheel. You might even be able to see Pine Hollow from the top of it!"

Jamie peeked up at Phil. "Could I see Nickel?"

Phil frowned. "Well, maybe. If Nickel's outside, of course."

"Well, okay," muttered Jamie, grabbing Lisa's hand again.

"You want to wear my space helmet?" Phil took off his pink hat and put it on Jamie's head.

Jamie looked up as the antennas wiggled above him.

Phil led the way to the Ferris wheel, showing Jamie the face-painting booth and the haunted house along the way. Jamie looked at everything, but nothing brought a smile to his face. "I want to ride the merry-go-round," he said again.

They bought tickets for the Ferris wheel. All five of them could fit into one of the double seats. Jamie sat between Carole and Lisa; Stevie and Phil faced them.

"Here we go," Phil said as the wheel began to lift them up.

"How's your sensitive stomach, Lisa?" Stevie asked, pretending to be afraid. "You're not going to barf, are you?"

"No." Lisa shook her head. "Sometimes I think my mother just dreams up things to worry about."

Bit by bit they rose higher, pausing as other people got on the ride. At the first stop they could see the tops of all the rides; then they could see the tops of all the trees; then suddenly they were at the top of the wheel and the whole countryside spread out before them like a green patchwork quilt.

"Where's Pine Hollow?" Jamie sat up straight and clutched the safety bar that held them in.

"It should be right over there." Phil squinted and pointed over Carole's left shoulder. Jamie turned and peered at the distant scenery.

"Can you see Nickel?" Stevie asked.

Jamie looked for a moment, then slumped back disappointedly in the seat. "No," he said as the Ferris wheel began to turn. "I want to ride the merry-go-round."

For three full rotations of the Ferris wheel, Jamie whined about the merry-go-round. Then the ride ended. Phil suggested they go buy Jamie some cotton candy. "Maybe it'll sweeten him up and he'll forget about the you-know-what," he whispered in Stevie's ear.

"I sure hope so," Stevie whispered back. "He's acting as bratty as my brothers."

They walked over to a snack booth and bought Jamie a giant cone of pink-and-blue cotton candy.

"Does it taste good, Jamie?" Stevie asked as they headed toward the Tilt-A-Whirl.

Jamie nodded with his mouth full. "But I still want to ride the merry-go-round."

"There are a lot of other neat rides here, Jamie," said Stevie. "Let's go try them out!"

So they spun twice on the Tilt-A-Whirl, turned upside down several times on the Phazer, and careened through at least three Typhoon rides. Stevie bought Jamie an Italian sausage sandwich while Carole and Lisa kept him well supplied with Sno-Kones and candy apples. All the while the only thing he talked about was the merry-go-round. Finally Phil took him to the milk bottle toss while The Saddle Club sat down under a tree to figure out what to do.

"I don't understand," grumbled Stevie. "We've taken Jamie on every ride here twice, we've fed him all the junk food the fair has to offer, and he still can't get over the merry-go-round."

"I know," Carole said. "We've done everything we can to distract him from it, but nothing seems to work. He's a sweet little boy at the stable, but here he's a real pain in the neck."

"I'm sorry," Lisa said sadly. "I had no idea he would act like this."

"It's not your fault," Stevie reassured her.

"Hey, everybody. Look what Jamie won!"

The girls looked up. Phil and Jamie were walking toward them. Jamie carried a huge brown teddy bear with a red bow around his neck.

"Wow, Jamie!" Carole said. "How did you win that?"

"He knocked down three bottles at the milk bottle toss," Phil explained with a big wink. "Jamie's got a great arm. The carnival guy was amazed!"

"That's terrific, Jamie!" Lisa said. "Aren't you happy?"

"Yes." Jamie nodded. "But I still want to ride the merry-go-round."

Crestfallen, the girls looked at each other. Everything they did was useless. Everything Phil did was useless. Jamie wanted to ride the merry-go-round, and nothing else would do.

"Wait," Stevie said, jumping up off the bench. "I've got an idea. Why don't we go back to the merry-go-round and see if they've fixed it?"

"All right!" Jamie's blue eyes sparkled.

Carole and Lisa glanced at each other, both wondering if this was such a great idea, but Jamie was already tugging Stevie and Phil toward the merry-go-round. They had no choice but to follow.

Hurrying past the gypsy fortune-teller and the dunking booth, they turned a corner and saw the merry-go-round, still dark and silent. The only thing different about it was that a carnival worker in denim coveralls was doing something to the motor with a wrench and an oil can.

"Sorry, Jamie," Phil said softly as tears came to the little boy's eyes. "Looks like it's still broken."

"Wait!" Stevie cried suddenly. "Stay right there. Don't move. I've just had a stroke of genius!"

Lisa and Carole stood beside Jamie and Phil and watched as Stevie ran to the merry-go-round. She threaded her way through the frozen horses and began talking to the man in the coveralls. He looked over at them once, scratched his

56

head, then shrugged his shoulders. Stevie pumped his hand madly, then motioned for everybody to come over.

"Are we going to ride?" Jamie asked excitedly.

"I don't know," Carole answered, wondering about Stevie's "stroke of genius."

"Jamie, this is Mr. Carter," Stevie said as they approached the ride. "He says the merry-go-round has a broken crankshaft and won't be fixed until the end of the week. But I explained to him that this is the only ride you really wanted to ride and how upset you are, and he says you can sit on whichever horse you want to."

"Really?" Jamie smiled for the first time that day.

Stevie nodded.

"Neat!" Jamie walked around the merry-go-round and studied each horse carefully. Finally he pointed to a coal black stallion wearing a red-and-gold saddle and rearing on its hind legs. "That one," he said.

"Exactly the one I would have chosen," said Stevie. They walked over to the horse and she lifted Jamie onto its back. "Pretty neat, huh?" She smiled.

"Yeah," Jamie said. He put his feet in the little stirrups and stroked the horse's wooden head. Then he closed his eyes and held the reins tight, pretending that the horse was galloping away with him. In just a moment, though, he opened his eyes again and looked at Stevie. "Can't the man make it work just for a little while?" he asked.

"I don't think so, Jamie," Stevie replied.

"Not even for just one turn?"

Stevie shook her head. "I think crankshafts take a long time to fix."

"Then I want to get off!"

"Okay." Stevie helped Jamie climb off the tall black horse. His legs wobbled a little as he walked to the edge of the platform, but he jumped off and landed squarely on the ground near Carole and Lisa. It was then, as Stevie was waving her thanks to Mr. Carter, that Jamie leaned over and made a retching sound. Just as Lisa turned to ask him what was wrong, every bit of food that he had eaten that day came up and landed in a multicolored puddle at his feet.

"Stevie!" Lisa cried. "Carole! Get me some water and a paper towel!" The two girls scurried off while Lisa picked Jamie up and carried him over to a shady tree. He looked pale and afraid.

"Oooh, my stomach hurts," he groaned, holding his middle.

"I know. I think you've had too many rides and way too much to eat," said Lisa gently.

Carole dashed up. "Here are some wet napkins," she said. "I couldn't find any paper towels."

"And here's some water and a soda," Stevie said, running up with Phil. "My mom always gives me a soda when I throw up."

Jamie rinsed his mouth out with the water while Lisa wiped the damp napkins over his face. Fortunately, his shirt was still clean. "Gosh, Jamie," she said after she had sponged his face off and wiped his forehead. "You feel awfully hot."

"I feel sick," moaned Jamie.

Carole bent down and felt his cheek. "He does feel hot, Lisa. Way too hot for just a warm day in early summer. I think he's got a fever."

"Really?" Stevie reached down and felt Jamie's other cheek. "Wow. I think Carole's right. Jamie doesn't have merry-go-round-itis. He's really sick!"

"What should we do now?" asked Phil.

"What time is it?" asked Lisa.

Stevie looked at her watch. "Three till three."

"Thank goodness," Lisa said with relief. "If we leave right now, my mother should be waiting by the time we get Jamie to the parking lot."

"Are you sure she'll be on time?" Phil asked.

"Oh, yes," replied Lisa. "My mother's never been late a day in her life."

THEY HURRIED OUT to the parking lot. Phil carried Jamie piggy-back while Stevie brought along the pink space helmet and the teddy bear. Lisa's mother was waiting for them exactly where she said she'd be.

"Hi," Mrs. Atwood called as they walked up to the car. "Did everyone have a good time?"

"Everyone but Jamie," said Lisa.

"What do you mean?" Mrs. Atwood frowned.

"I think he's sick, Mom," Lisa replied worriedly. "I mean really sick. He's hot and he threw up."

Jamie climbed off Phil's back and crawled into the car. Mrs. Atwood turned around and felt his forehead with the back of her hand. "He's definitely coming down with something," she said. "He's hot and his face looks flushed." She gave Jamie a sympathetic smile. "Honey, does your tummy hurt?"

Jamie nodded and curled himself up in the far corner of the backseat. "They didn't even have a merry-go-round that worked," he complained in a wounded voice.

"Oh, I'm so sorry." Mrs. Atwood stroked his hair gently. "Lisa, why don't you sit in the back with Jamie and keep him company? Carole, you and Stevie can ride up front with me."

"Thanks, Mrs. Atwood, but Phil and I are going to stay a little longer," Stevie explained. "Mrs. Marsten's going to give me a ride home later. My mom said it was okay." She stashed the teddy bear and the pink space helmet in the backseat beside Lisa. "I'll see you guys tomorrow," she said as Carole climbed in beside Mrs. Atwood. "Jamie, I hope you feel better."

"Yeah, Jamie," Phil added. "Me too. Take care of yourself."

Frowning, Jamie turned his head away from them and stared out the window.

"You two have fun," said Carole as Mrs. Atwood started the car. "See you tomorrow, Stevie."

Stevie and Phil waved, then headed back to the fair, hand in hand. Carole turned around and looked at Lisa and Jamie. Jamie's face was deep pink and his eyelids fluttered as if he was about to fall asleep.

"Gosh." Carole frowned. "Maybe we shouldn't have given him all that junk food. We fed him everything they were selling at the fair. Cotton candy, funnel cakes, Sno-Kones, and none of it had any kind of protein or vitamins. No wonder he threw up!"

"I don't know," said Lisa, brushing Jamie's bangs away from his clammy forehead. His eyes were closed, and he moaned sleepily. "I think he felt bad all morning. Remember how he was whining about the merry-go-round all day? That's just not like him. I don't think he would have acted like that if he hadn't been sick to begin with." She sighed. "I think all that junk food just made him feel a whole lot worse."

Carole shrugged. "I suppose. But who would have guessed he was sick? I thought he was just upset about the merry-go-round."

"Wait a minute," Lisa said suddenly, squinting at a tiny red spot on Jamie's neck. She pulled down the collar of his shirt, then lifted up the front of it. His stomach was covered in pin-sized red blisters. She looked up at Carole in alarm.

"Unless Jamie's got some kind of weird blister-shaped sunburn under his shirt, I think he's got chicken pox!"

"What?" cried Carole.

"Mom!" Lisa tapped her mother on the shoulder. "Can you look at this?"

Mrs. Atwood pulled off to the side of the road and stopped the car. She leaned over the seat and ran one finger gently over Jamie's blotchy stomach. "Well, that's exactly what they looked like when you and your brother had them," she said.

"I believe you're right, Lisa. I think this child has chicken pox."

"Oh no," Carole groaned. "He must have caught it at the stable. Remember when we talked to Max about Jamie riding Nickel? Somehow he must have caught it from Maxi."

"This is all my fault!" cried Lisa. "I was the one who suggested bringing Jamie to Pine Hollow in the first place. If I had just stayed at his house and baby-sat him there, this never would have happened. Now I have to tell his mother. I feel terrible!"

"I'm sure Jamie's mother will understand," Mrs. Atwood said as she pulled back onto the highway. "Illnesses are just part of raising children. Parents have to be prepared for things like this to happen."

"But if it hadn't been for me, it might not have happened for a long, long time," Lisa replied miserably.

Jamie squirmed on the seat, then leaned his head against Lisa's shoulder. By the time they pulled into the Bacons' driveway, he was sound asleep. Lisa gathered him up in her arms as Mrs. Atwood reached behind the seat and opened the door.

"Do you want some help, Lisa?" Carole asked.

"Yes. Could you bring in his teddy bear and the space helmet? And then hang around and give me some moral support?" Lisa dreaded telling Mrs. Bacon that she had taken her son out for a wonderful time at the fair and brought him back with an upset stomach and chicken pox.

"Sure." Carole fished Jamie's prizes from the back of the car while Lisa carried Jamie against her shoulder.

When Mrs. Bacon came to the door, Lisa told her the story. "Then, when I cleaned him up, he felt awfully hot, and on the way over here, I noticed all these red spots on his stomach." She swallowed. "Mrs. Bacon, I think Jamie might have chicken pox. The daughter of the owner of Pine Hollow has it, and I think Jamie might have been exposed to it when I took him over there on Monday."

"Oh no," said Mrs. Bacon. She took Jamie to the sofa and laid him down. He looked at his mother and again groaned sleepily. She pulled his shirt up and inspected his stomach. Just as Lisa had said, pinpoints of red prickled his stomach and chest. "Look." Mrs. Bacon pointed to three new spots on Jamie's cheek. "They're beginning to pop out on his face, too." She looked at Lisa. "I think you're right. I think he does have chicken pox."

"I'm so sorry," said Lisa, giving Carole a panic-stricken look. "I would never have taken him to Pine Hollow if I'd thought it would give him chicken pox!"

Though Mrs. Bacon's eyes were still full of concern, she smiled at Lisa and put an arm around her shoulders. "I know that, Lisa. And I don't want you to worry about that for a minute. Jamie couldn't have caught chicken pox at Pine Hollow. It takes a lot longer than two days for a disease like that to develop." She looked at Carole. "He probably got it from one of his classmates at Fenton Hall before school was out. Poor little guy. He was so excited about going to the fair with you two and Stevie."

Though Lisa realized she wasn't to blame, she still felt awful. "Is there anything we can do to help?" she asked.

Mrs. Bacon thought a moment. "Well, it would be wonderful if you could help me get Jamie settled in his room."

The girls followed Mrs. Bacon as she carried Jamie down the hall to his bedroom. Lisa pulled the covers down on his bed while Carole arranged the space helmet on the teddy bear's head and sat it in a rocking chair. Mrs. Bacon untied Jamie's sneakers, laid him on the bed, and went into the hall to call the doctor's office.

Just as Mrs. Bacon began telling the nurse his symptons, Jamie opened his eyes.

"Hi." He blinked at Lisa and Carole, still groggy from his nap. "How come you're here?"

"Remember getting sick at the fair?" Lisa asked.

Jamie nodded.

"Remember getting into my mom's car?"

He nodded again.

"Well, you fell asleep after that. We brought you home and put you to bed. Your mom's just called the doctor."

Mrs. Bacon hung up the phone and came back into the room. "Well, Jamie, it seems that Lisa was right. You've got chicken pox. Dr. McLean says you need to stay in bed and get plenty of rest."

Jamie yawned.

"Do you think you could go back to sleep now?"

He nodded. Mrs. Bacon tucked the covers over him and kissed him on the cheek. "Then say good-bye to Lisa and Carole."

"Bye," Jamie murmured. "Thanks for taking me to the fair."

Lisa smiled. "Bye, Jamie. I hope you feel better real soon."

"Let me see these girls to the door, Jamie, and I'll be right back." Mrs. Bacon motioned for Lisa and Carole to follow her out of the room.

The girls tiptoed out into the hall. "Thanks so much for all your help," Mrs. Bacon whispered as she closed Jamie's door. "I know you tried your best to see that he had a good time today."

"I just hope he gets better in a hurry," Lisa said as they walked to the front door.

Mrs. Bacon turned to Lisa. "The doctor says Jamie will have to stay at home until he stops breaking out, so I'll have to stay home with him. I guess I won't be needing a baby-sitter for a while."

"Oh." Lisa's heart sank. In all the excitement, it had not occurred to her that Jamie's bout of chicken pox would mean the end of her baby-sitting job.

Mrs. Bacon opened the door for them. "But I'll be sure and call you when he's well." She gave Carole a smile. "Thanks again to both of you for taking such good care of him."

"You're welcome, Mrs. Bacon," Lisa said. "Tell Jamie we hope he feels better soon."

Mrs. Bacon closed the door. Carole and Lisa walked slowly down the walkway.

"There goes my baby-sitting job," Lisa said dejectedly. "Now I don't know where I'm going to get the money I promised to give my parents for my riding lessons."

"Oh no," said Carole. "That's terrible. Couldn't you find somebody else to baby-sit?"

"Sure, but it'll take time to find another job. Most people already have their baby-sitters lined up for the summer. I need the money now!" She looked at Carole. "What if I have to quit taking lessons at Pine Hollow?"

"Maybe your parents could extend you some credit," Carole suggested.

"I don't know." Lisa shook her head. "That wasn't part of our original agreement."

"Well, there must be tons of other kids who need baby-sitters. Don't worry. If another job doesn't come along, The Saddle Club will help you figure something out."

Lisa stared at the ground. No job, no money, and maybe no more riding lessons. Her summer was only three days old, and already it was ruined!

"IT'S ABOUT TIME you guys got here!" Stevie looked up from her cubby as Carole and Lisa walked into the locker room.

The two girls frowned at each other. "Our class doesn't start for half an hour," said Lisa. "Did we have a Saddle Club meeting that we forgot about?"

"No," Stevie replied impatiently. "I didn't have a chance to call you last night, and I just wanted to find out what happened to Jamie after you got him home from the fair!"

"Oh, that," said Carole. "Well, the famous Dr. Atwood here made the correct diagnosis in the backseat of the car."

"Really?" Stevie looked at Lisa. "And?"

"And Jamie has chicken pox," Lisa reported glumly. "And now the famous Dr. Atwood is out of a baby-sitting job."

"Oh no," groaned Stevie. "That was your riding lesson money, too. What are you going to do?"

"I don't know." Lisa hung her change purse up in her cubby. "I called all my old clients last night, and everybody's either out of town, or at camp, or too old now to be baby-sat. I'm going to have to start from square one."

"Well, I'm not surprised," said Stevie.

"Thanks a lot," Lisa said.

"No, I mean about Jamie's chicken pox. It's going around all over town. Michael's friend Shawn has seventy-five pox on his face alone."

"Yuck." Carole grimaced. "That's gross."

"Yes, and don't forget about poor little Maxi. She's been itching for over a week. We should have thought of chicken pox the moment Jamie threw up."

Carole frowned. "I don't know, Stevie. There was no reason for us to think Jamie had it. After all, we'd fed him everything we could think of and taken him on every ride they had. That might have made anybody sick." She pulled her shoulder-length black hair back in a ponytail. "Gosh, we're not doctors or nurses or anything. We aren't even mothers."

"I'm not sure we deserve to be mothers after the fair disaster," Lisa said.

"What do you mean?" asked Stevie.

Lisa shook her head. "Stevie, all we did yesterday was bribe Jamie. Once he started acting so bratty about the merry-go-round, we just caved in and bribed him to be happy with junk food and carnival rides. That's no way to treat a cranky child. Even I know that."

"I don't think that's so bad," Stevie protested. "I mean, even if we didn't know Jamie was sick and even if bribery isn't on the top-ten list of things parents ought to do, it's pretty neat when you're the one being bribed." Stevie gave them an impish grin. "If Jamie hadn't been sick, he'd have been having the time of his life!"

Carole and Lisa looked at each other and burst out laughing.

Only Stevie could come up with logic like that!

The girls continued getting ready for their riding lesson. Carole changed into her boots and put her mythology book in the top of her cubby.

"Are you still reading that?" Stevie asked in amazement.

"Oh, yes," Carole answered. "It's gotten even better. Now Pegasus and Bellerophon are starting to fight the Amazons for King Iobates, but he's getting suspicious that—"

Suddenly Max walked past the locker room. "Hi, girls," he called as he adjusted the bit of a new bridle. "How's it going?"

"Hi, Max," they all said together.

"How's Maxi doing?" asked Carole. "Is she feeling any better?"

"She's just beginning to," Max replied, leaning against the door as he rebuckled the bridle's cavesson. "Last night Deborah and I actually got four uninterrupted hours of sleep.

Maxi's a lot less fussy, but she looks a lot worse—like someone painted red dots on every inch of her." He picked up a bubble gum wrapper from the floor, then scratched his head. "It seems like with chicken pox, the worse you look, the closer you are to getting better."

"That's the way I feel every time I get a cold," Stevie said. "I have to feel like I'm about to croak before anyone even notices I'm sick. By the time anybody has any sympathy for me, I'm almost well." She paused and loosened the collar of her shirt. "In fact, I'm feeling kind of hot in here right now. I sure would be grateful if either of my dear friends was to say how sorry they were I was feeling bad."

"Oh, poor sick Stevie," Carole wailed dramatically. She picked up a saddle pad and began to fan Stevie's face. "Does this help cool you off a little? Shall I peel you a grape for some extra vitamin C?"

"I bet I know something that will make her feel better," Lisa said, laughing. "We can take her back to the fair and buy her a funnel cake and an extra-long ride on the merry-go-round! They might even let her ride without a safety strap."

"Well, you'd better nurse your partner in crime back to health soon," Max said as he began to stride down the hall. "Your riding class starts in fifteen minutes."

"Yikes!" Stevie leaped to her feet. "We'd better tack up fast!"

Carole chuckled. "That's the wonder drug for Stevie Lake. Just say the words *riding class* and she's cured immediately!"

The girls tacked up their horses quickly and met with the

rest of their class in the outdoor ring. Everyone made a big circle around Max, who stood in the center.

"Okay, everybody," he said, shading his eyes from the glare of the sun. "Before we mount up I want one of our riders to share with us some of the things she learned when she spent the day with our equine vet, Judy Barker. Carole, would you ask Stevie to hold your horse while you talk to the class?"

Carole handed Starlight's reins to Stevie and walked over to Max. She hadn't known he was going to call on her like this! Butterflies began to flit in her stomach, but she stood in the center of the ring and tried to remember all she had learned with Judy.

She cleared her throat and spoke loudly enough for everyone to hear. "Tuesday, Judy and I visited a stable that was run by people who have recently moved here from California. They're nice people who don't want their horses to get sick, but they didn't realize that they weren't keeping their stable clean enough." Carole remembered how Lady Jane and Joker and Spirit had been suffering at the Albergini farm.

"Their manure wasn't far enough away from the barn, so flies hatched in it and then bit the horses. They didn't know to fill all the low places where water could stand, so the barn was swarming with mosquitoes. They hadn't sprayed their barn or stalls with any kind of insecticide, so one of their horses was infested with lice. All these insects can cause serious diseases in horses."

A wave of "ugh" and "gross" went up from the whole class. Carole shifted on her feet and continued.

"The good news, though, is that Judy was able to show them how to clean up their place, and all the horses are going to be fine."

She smiled over at Max. "Even better news is that we don't have any of those problems at Pine Hollow. There is no standing water; Red trucks the manure a safe distance away; and we've all seen the insecticide truck come here every month." Carole couldn't think of anything else to say, so she began to return to Starlight. Suddenly she remembered one last thing. She trotted back to the center of the ring and added, "And we have several terrific new bug zappers that can kill anything within a hundred feet."

With that, Carole hurried back to her horse. The other riders laughed and applauded as Max returned to the center of the ring.

"Thanks, Carole," he said. "But I think you've given Pine Hollow too much credit. We do take pest control very seriously, but we've also been very lucky. Even the cleanest, most careful stables can get invaded by pests. It's our job as riders to give flies and worms as little chance as possible to survive in a stable, and if they do get in, to get rid of them immediately."

Max eyed each rider. "Remember, there's no such thing as a pest-free barn, just as there's no guarantee that the child of the most loving parents in the world won't get sick."

After Max finished his lecture, the class mounted up.

"Okay," he called. "We're going to do a little dressage work today and practice the counter-canter, but first we need to warm up. Carole, since you gave us such a good report on horseflies, would you and Starlight lead the class in a posting trot?"

Carole nodded, proud that Max had chosen her. She pulled Starlight out of line and turned him to the right, urging him into a trot. For about three strides, he obeyed; then he broke into a canter. When Carole tried to pull him back to a trot, he stopped altogether. Two girls on the other side of the ring laughed.

"Starlight!" Carole whispered. "Come on! Don't act like such a nut!" She collected herself and tried again. Starlight did the same thing as before: trot, canter, then a dead stop. Carole felt her face grow hot with embarrassment as the other riders stared at her. She turned into the circle and trotted over to Max.

"Max, I think he needs to run a little bit before we do any work. He's got a bad case of spring fever this year."

"That's okay, Carole. It's good that you know your mount so well. Take him over to the paddock for a good run and come back when he's ready."

"Thanks." Carole smiled gratefully.

She rode Starlight out of the ring as Stevie and Belle began leading the exercise. "Come on, Starlight," Carole said as they entered the big paddock. "Let's get all the kinks out so we can get back to class."

74

Starlight pranced and fidgeted at first, but he settled down when Carole allowed him to canter. They did one circuit of the paddock, and then Carole let him gallop. His long legs stretched out and the fence posts flew by, just as fast as they had before. Again Starlight seemed happiest when he was racing at full speed, and again Carole found herself dreaming about what it must be like to ride a horse that had wings as well as four strong legs.

When Starlight's breathing became heavy, Carole slowed him to a trot. "There," she said, giving him a pat. Those kinks must be worked out by now." They did one cool-down lap of the paddock, then reentered the ring. Max was just explaining the counter-canter exercise.

"I want all of you to canter your horses through the serpentine without changing leads. That means they'll be cantering with the right lead half the time and the wrong lead the other half of the time. It'll feel weird to you at first, but it's an excellent way to keep both you and your mount supple and in tune with each other. Understand?" All the riders nodded.

"Okay. Lisa, would you lead off, please? Just ride through this zigzag course and keep giving the signals for a left lead."

Carole guided Starlight to a place at the end of the line and watched as Lisa and Prancer led off the exercise. Moving at an easy canter, Lisa worked her way down the ring, Prancer always leading with her left foreleg.

"Good!" Max called when they finished. "Okay, next rider, follow her!"

The next rider was Stevie on Belle; then the third rider joined in. By the time Starlight and Carole joined the line, most of the other riders had finished and were waiting to see what she and Starlight were going to do.

"Okay, boy, here we go," Carole said softly.

At first Starlight lurched forward in a bounding canter. Carole reined him in, and he continued in a more collected gait. His canter was smooth, and though he wanted to change his lead, he obeyed her signals to maintain it. Carole felt a warm glow of pride as they zigzagged perfectly down the length of the ring. She had been right about what was wrong with Starlight all along, and she had also been right about what to do about it. It was just the way Max said: A good horse owner knew what was best for her horse.

Max finished the lesson by having them ride in large circles to practice a turn called the volt. Then he had them cool their horses down. Carole guided Starlight over beside Lisa and Stevie.

"Hey, you looked great out there," Carole said to Lisa.

"Thanks," Lisa said. "I was kind of nervous. I kept hoping I would remember how to ask for a left lead." She laughed and gave Prancer a pat on the neck. "I guess Prancer knew what I was asking for."

"Phew!" Stevie exclaimed. "Don't you guys think it's hot today?" She pulled her shirttail out and fanned cool air on her stomach.

"Not really," said Carole. "But mostly I've been flying around the paddock on Starlight."

Stevie wiped the sweat from her forehead. "I've got a good idea. Why don't we untack everybody fast and call an emergency Saddle Club meeting at TD's? Wouldn't a lime sherbet freeze with coconut and chocolate taste good right now?"

"Well, I could maybe go for a plain old hot fudge sundae," said Lisa. "But what's our emergency?"

"Uh, we can dream up alternative air-conditioning plans," Stevie suggested with a grin.

"Huh?" said Carole.

"You know. Ways The Saddle Club can stay cool this summer. Lots of swimming, wading in the creek . . ."

"Trips to TD's?" Carole laughed.

"Right," said Stevie.

"Sounds good to me!"

"Great!" Stevie turned Belle toward the stable. "Last one ready to go to TD's is a rotten egg!"

Though of course the girls dismounted and walked their horses back into the stable, they moved as quickly as they could. Carole could hear Stevie whistling as she untacked Belle.

"I promise I'll give you a bath and the grooming to end all groomings tomorrow, Starlight," Carole vowed as she pulled the saddle off her sweaty horse. She put up his tack and quickly curried him, running a brush over him just enough to get the sweat off his skin. She filled his water bucket with fresh water and gave him two armloads of hay. He nickered with contentment as he settled down to munch his snack.

"It won't always be like this, Starlight," she said. "Just as soon as everything settles down and I finish with my Pegasus project, I promise you'll be the only horse I think about for the rest of the summer!"

"I'm almost ready," Stevie taunted from Belle's stall.

"Bye, Starlight." Carole rubbed him gently behind the ears before she hurried out of the stall. "I'll see you tomorrow!"

"AHHHHH!" STEVIE SLID contentedly into their usual booth at TD's. The ice cream shop was deliciously cool. "I can't believe you guys aren't hot. I've been roasting all day."

"Poor Stevie," Carole sympathized. "Some ice cream should cool you off fast."

Stevie sat back in the booth and gazed at the ceiling, pondering her choices. "Let's see . . . What sounds good today?"

"I'm sure you'll come up with something," Lisa said, giggling.

The girls studied the menu, though they knew it by heart. Finally the waitress came over to take their order.

"Let me guess," she said, pulling out her pad. She looked at Lisa. "You'll have a scoop of chocolate with marshmallow sauce. Your one friend there will have a double cone with pistachio and strawberry. What your other friend who's fanning herself with the menu will have, I hesitate to even ask."

Everyone looked at Stevie, who had a reputation for strange and exotic ice cream creations. The waitress waited, her pencil poised.

"Ummmm, I think I'll have one scoop of double Dutch chocolate and one scoop of banana raspberry with pineapple sauce on top."

The waitress shook her head and scribbled down Stevie's order.

"And since I'm feeling a little under the weather, could you put a couple of green cherries on top, too?" Stevie looked up pitifully. "Please?"

"Coming up," the waitress said as she walked back behind the counter.

"Well, that should certainly make you feel better, Stevie." Carole crossed her eyes at the thought of Stevie's latest dessert.

"I think it would put me under the table," Lisa said with a laugh. "Almost like having chicken pox."

"Do you remember having chicken pox?" Carole asked.

"Sure," said Lisa. "I was in the first grade. My teacher discovered a rash on my neck and called my mother. She came rushing to the school like I had diphtheria or something." She shuddered at the memory. "I was so embarrassed."

"I had them in the first grade, too," recalled Carole. "My dad was stationed at Beaufort, South Carolina, and we lived in Marine Corps housing. I remember my mother would come into my room every afternoon with a milk shake for me, and we'd play on the bed. She'd read to me or make these really neat origami animals." She smiled. Her mother had died several months before the girls had formed The Saddle Club. For a long time Carole had been very sad, but now she mostly remembered the good times she and her mother had enjoyed together. "I remember itching some, but mostly I remember how much fun it was to be with her."

Stevie frowned. "All I remember is Alex looking speckled and griping all the time. My mother had to bathe him with some kind of oatmeal soap, so our whole bathroom smelled like a giant cookie. It made me hungry."

"Didn't you have to take the oatmeal bath, too?" Lisa asked.

Stevie shrugged. "I guess not. If I did, I don't remember it. I think Alex had a much worse case than I did."

Just then the waitress arrived with their orders. Along with three small glasses of water, she set a dish of chocolate ice cream in front of Lisa, handed Carole a double-scoop cone, and then placed a huge brown, yellow, and magenta concoction in front of Stevie, complete with two green cherries on top. "There you are." She gave Stevie a pained look. "Enjoy."

"Yum!" said Stevie, digging in.

Carole and Lisa watched as she took her first bite.

"Well?" Carole asked. "Do you think this dish will restore you to health?"

Stevie nodded with a grin. "I'm beginning to feel better already."

Lisa swirled a spoonful of her chocolate ice cream in the marshmallow sauce. "You know, I've been thinking about Jamie and the fair. It's too bad he had such an awful time. He's really such a sweet little kid. And his mother said he'd really been looking forward to going with us."

"That's true," agreed Carole. "What's bad is that everything we tried to do to make him feel better only made him feel worse."

Stevie popped a green cherry in her mouth. "You mean feeding him all that delicious food and taking him on all those neat rides?"

Carole nodded. "We meant well, but I think we blew it."

"I wonder if there's anything we could do now to make him feel better," Lisa said. "I mean, now that he's sick at home and can't go anywhere."

"We could bring him something to eat from here," Stevie suggested. Her eyes suddenly brightened. "I know! I could invent a dish and name it in his honor!"

"Thanks, Stevie. That's sweet, but we need to do something that will make him feel better, not make him sick all over again," said Lisa.

Carole snapped her fingers. "I know. We could go shopping and try to find him a get-well present. You know, something he could play with and keep."

"That's a great idea!" Lisa said. Buying Jamie a get-well present wouldn't help her save money, but he definitely needed cheering up.

"Yeah." Stevie nodded. "That would work. But when can all of us go shopping?"

"How about Saturday, after Horse Wise?" suggested Carole.

"Fine with me." Lisa turned to Stevie. "Can you go then?"

She nodded vigorously, since her mouth was full of double Dutch chocolate. She swallowed her ice cream, then took a sip of water. "Since we're discussing the fair," she began, "let me tell you what happened with Phil after you guys took Jamie home."

"Oh, Stevie, we can guess what happened after we took Jamie home. You and Phil had a marvelous time under the romantic midway lights and pledged each other your undying love on top of the Ferris wheel," said Carole.

"Yeah, Stevie." Lisa giggled. "We can fill in the blanks ourselves. We don't want to pry into your love life."

"No, no, no!" Stevie cried. "That's not what I'm talking about. Remember the dunking booth they had there for charity? Remember how all different sorts of people were climbing in and acting crazy to see if their friends could dunk them in the water?"

Lisa and Carole nodded.

"Well, I convinced Phil to do that!"

"To sit in the dunking booth?" Lisa asked.

Stevie grinned. "I told him it was for charity, and even if he did get all wet, it would be for a good cause." She cackled. "When he climbed out he looked like a drowned rat. At first he was mad, but then I reminded him of how much money he'd made for charity. Then I told him I wouldn't make him pay up the five-dollar bet he'd just lost. By the time the evening was over, I think he kind of enjoyed being soaked!"

"That's really funny!" said Lisa.

"Yeah," Carole agreed. "But it sounds like poor wet Phil deserves more sympathy than you do!"

The girls finished their ice cream and paid their bill. "Anybody want to come over for a swim?" Stevie asked as they walked back out into the sunny afternoon.

"No thanks," Lisa replied. "I need to go home." She rolled her eyes. "My mom wants to show me some new colors she's picked out for my room."

"I'm going to walk over to the library," said Carole. "I've got some more work to do on my Pegasus project."

Stevie and Lisa laughed. "You'd better hurry, Carole," Lisa teased. "You've only got eleven more weeks to finish it."

Carole grinned and waved. "Don't worry. I'll do my best," she called. "See you Saturday!"

After a twenty-minute walk across town, Carole came to the main public library—an old redbrick building next to the Willow Creek Town Hall. She slowly climbed up the broad stone steps, pausing to admire the two huge granite lions that stood guard at the big double doors. Inside the foyer, a tall young man with curly blond hair sat behind the returns desk, rearranging a stack of children's books.

"Excuse me," Carole said just above a whisper. "Could you tell me where I could find the mythology section?"

The librarian looked up and smiled. "Sure. Follow me and I'll show you."

He walked over to a far corner of the library. Carole tried to follow him quickly, but her barn boots thumped so noisily on the wooden floors that she finally had to give up and creep along on tiptoe. Even so, people looked up from their reading as she passed. *The next time I come here*, she thought, *I won't come directly from TD's and Pine Hollow.*

The librarian stood waiting for her, smiling. "The mythology collection starts here," he said, pointing to a large red book high above Carole's head, "and ends here." He pulled out a short fat volume at the end of a row two shelves down.

"Wow." Carole looked at the bulging shelves. "That's a lot of books."

"Is there a particular type of mythology you're interested in?" he asked. "Greek? Norse? Chinese?"

"Greek," Carole replied. "I'm studying the myth of Pegasus and Bellerophon."

"Ahhh," the young man said knowingly. "That's a good one. Try this book." He pulled out a tattered blue book with Greek-looking gold letters on the cover. "It covers Pegasus and Bellerophon better than any of the others." He gave her a funny smile. "It's almost as if you're really there."

"Thanks," said Carole. "Thanks a lot."

Carole sat down at a small desk and opened the book. Just as the librarian had said, it had many pages devoted to the adventures of Pegasus and Bellerophon, each with wonderful full-color pictures. She scanned down to where her old paperback had left off, then began to read.

After Bellerophon had defeated the Amazons, King Iobates decided to give him the hand of his daughter in marriage. There was a wedding feast, and for a while Bellerophon and his bride were very happy.

Before long, though, Bellerophon became dissatisfied with such a quiet, peaceful life. He remembered all the hours he had spent flying on Pegasus' back and all the adventures they had shared together. "I'm just as brave as any of the gods," he said one day. "I'll bet if Pegasus flew me to Mount Olympus, Zeus would make me immortal. Then I could fight dragons and slay monsters forever."

So Bellerophon called his faithful friend Pegasus. With a neigh and a rush of white wings, the huge stallion landed at Bellerophon's feet. The young man climbed on his back and said, "Take me to Mount Olympus, Pegasus. Take me to Father Zeus!"

At first Pegasus refused to go, but Bellerophon insisted, jabbing him sternly with his heels. The great horse reared once, then spread his wings, and away they flew, faster and higher, until the golden slopes of Mount Olympus glittered through misty lavender clouds. Higher and higher yet they flew, Bellerophon calling, "Father Zeus! It's your son, Bellerophon!"

All at once there was a blinding flash of lightning and a rumble of thunder. A deep, foreboding voice rolled through the heavens, saying, "Come no further, mortal! Turn away!" But Bellerophon refused to turn Pegasus back. They flew onward until suddenly the sky grew inky black except for a single particle of light that raced toward them. Bellerophon wept tears of joy. Father Zeus must have recognized him and sent a light to show them the way! But the light grew bigger and bigger and then began to buzz like a million bees. Bellerophon realized with horror that Zeus had not sent a beacon to guide him but rather a gadfly to sting Pegasus away!

"No!" Bellerophon screamed as the fly buzzed nearer and nearer. "No!"

But it was too late. The fly stung Pegasus viciously on his flank. The huge horse reared in agony, and off tumbled Bellerophon, away from Mount Olympus, falling forever down into the darkness of the earth below.

"Excuse me? Are you okay?"

Carole sat up and blinked. The librarian knelt beside her, his eyebrows knotted with worry. "Yes, I'm fine," she said. "Why?"

The young man spoke in a soft voice. "Well, I was over

there reshelving some books when I heard you call out, 'No!' I looked over here and you had your head down on the desk with your eyes closed." He gave her a kind smile. "I think you must have fallen asleep on Pegasus."

"Oh no!" Carole was mortified.

The librarian laughed. "It's okay. Nobody heard you but me. I'm just glad you're all right."

Carole gazed down at the book. The pictures seemed to glow before her eyes. It occurred to her that this was the most unusual visit to the library she'd ever had.

The librarian got up and continued to reshelve his books. "Did you finish it?" he asked.

"What?" Carole replied.

"The story."

"Uh, no. Not quite."

"Go ahead, then. It's got a terrific ending."

Carole rubbed her eyes and began reading where she'd left off, or at least where she'd begun talking in her sleep.

Zeus, however, took pity on Pegasus, the brave and willing horse that had served Bellerophon so loyally. He soothed the sting of the gadfly with nectar and ambrosia and brought Pegasus to live among the gods on Mount Olympus. Pegasus had many grand adventures with the other gods there, and after many years they honored his courage and loyalty by placing him in the sky. Today he soars through the heavens still, in the stars of the constellation Pegasus.

For a moment Carole just sat at the desk and stared at the book. It was a perfect story with a perfect ending. Pegasus, the most loyal and magnificent horse in all creation, got to live in heaven, while Bellerophon, who probably couldn't have done anything at all without a whole lot of help from Pegasus and the gods, got booted out of Mount Olympus before he got his foot in the door. *Served him right*, thought Carole. *His head was getting entirely too big for his helmet.*

Carole put the book back on the shelf. She had more than enough information to finish her project now. She would have to think hard about how to develop it, but she was sure she could come up with something really special to start off the new school year.

Slowly she walked back to the entrance of the library.

"Well?" said the young librarian. "Did you finish it?"

Carole nodded and smiled.

"What did you think?"

"I thought it was perfect," Carole replied. "The most beautiful flying horse gets to live with the gods."

The librarian raised one eyebrow. "True, but didn't you feel just a little sorry for poor old Bellerophon?"

Carole frowned. "In a way. But only because he never realized how much he owed Pegasus and the gods. It was as if he was so sure of himself that he could never really see the truth. Zeus even warned him not to try to land on Mount Olympus, but he still wouldn't listen."

The librarian nodded. "That's absolutely right. The gods

were never particularly kind to any mortal, and they almost never invited anybody to come up and live on Mount Olympus."

Carole looked out the window and saw her bus coming down the block. "Oops," she said. "I've got to go or I'll miss my bus. Thanks for all your help!"

"My pleasure." The young man smiled.

9

"HERE YOU ARE, kiddo." Colonel Hanson pulled into the Pine Hollow parking lot early Saturday morning. "I hope you have a great time today."

"Thanks for the ride, Dad." Carole smiled at her father. He looked so handsome in his Marine Corps uniform that she was almost tempted to go with him and watch the dress parade, but today was Horse Wise, and Judy Barker was going to talk about summertime horse care. That was important, and Carole figured if she was serious about being Judy's assistant, she'd better not miss it. She unbuckled her seat belt. "I'll see you at home later this afternoon."

"Right," said Colonel Hanson. "And don't forget to tell Stevie that joke I heard." He chuckled. "I think she'll really get a kick out of it."

"Okay, Dad," Carole promised dutifully. Stevie and her father shared a love of corny old jokes. Colonel Hanson seemed to have an endless supply of them, although Carole thought he had really scraped the bottom of the barrel with this one. "Bye!" She smiled and waved to her father, then hurried on into the stable.

Stevie and Lisa were sitting by their cubbies. "Hi, guys," Carole called. "Ready for Horse Wise?"

"I am," said Lisa.

"Gosh, Carole," Stevie said, grinning and giving Lisa a wink. "We didn't know if you were coming or not. We thought you might have decided to spend the whole weekend in the library, doing extra research on Pegasus."

Carole smiled as she remembered her visit to the library. "Actually, I found everything I needed yesterday afternoon. Now I just have to write my report." She threw her sneakers into her cubby. "Hey, Stevie, my dad sent you a new joke."

"Really?" Stevie grinned with anticipation. "What?"

"You'd better sit down," Carole warned. "It's a real killer."

Stevie laughed. "I *am* sitting down."

"Okay." Carole finished lacing one boot and took a deep breath. "Here goes. Why wouldn't the skeleton cross the road?"

Stevie frowned for a long moment, then shrugged. "I give up. Why?"

"Because he didn't have any guts!"

"Arrrggggh," Lisa groaned, but Stevie nearly fell off the bench laughing.

"That's a really good one," she hooted. "That's the best one I've heard in a long time!"

"Oh, Stevie," Carole said. She and Lisa looked at each other and shook their heads as Stevie began laughing all over again.

Just then some other riders passed by the locker room, trooping toward the front entrance. "We need to go," said Lisa. "Horse Wise is about to start."

The girls hurried outside and seated themselves with the other riders under a maple tree just beyond the riding ring. Max and Judy Barker stood before the group with an array of horse equipment laid out on a red blanket. When everyone had sat down, Max stepped forward and began to speak.

"Riders, today the first half of our Horse Wise meeting will be serious—Judy is going to talk to us about how seasonal changes can affect the health and care of your horses. For the second half of the meeting, we'll mount up and have a little fun. So give Judy a nice round of applause, and I'll turn the meeting over to her."

Everyone clapped for Judy, who shook hands with Max and stepped to one side of the red blanket.

"How many of you have figured out that it's summertime?" she asked, taking off her cowboy hat and pretending to wipe sweat from her forehead.

Everyone laughed and held up a hand.

"Well, your horses have figured that out, too. And just as you don't have to stay in school all summer, the horses don't have to stay in the stable. In the summer they like to get out and graze in the breezy pasture instead of staying cooped up in a hot barn." Judy looked at the group. "Can anybody tell me what that means to them foodwise?"

A little girl in the front row raised her hand. "That they'll eat a late breakfast and snack later at night?"

Everybody laughed again. Judy smiled. "Well, you're almost right. Unlike you guys, they won't eat pizza at midnight, but they will get up early and graze until they're put in the barn at night. Their diet will change, too. Just like a big bowl of hot soup wouldn't sound too good to us on the Fourth of July, in the summer horses like more grass and oats and less hay and corn." Judy questioned the group again. "Can anybody tell me what else is different in the summertime for a horse?"

"They don't have to wear blankets at night," May Grover responded.

"That's right, May. What else?"

Jasmine James waved her hand. "All their winter hair falls out."

"Right. And who can tell me what happens when a horse's winter coat falls out?" Judy waited for an answer, but nobody seemed to know. "Anybody?" she asked again. No one responded.

"Okay. I'll show you, but first I need a volunteer horse from the audience." Judy's gaze fell on The Saddle Club. "Carole, would you bring Starlight out here for a demonstration?"

"Sure." Carole jumped to her feet, delighted to be chosen but wondering if Starlight would behave. Surely he wouldn't dare act up at a demonstration with Judy Barker. Carole raced to the barn and clipped a lead line on Starlight. "Please be good, Starlight," she whispered as she led him back out beside Judy.

"Thanks," Judy said softly. She took Starlight's halter and addressed the riders. "When a horse loses his winter coat and spends a lot more time outside, he becomes a virtual fast-food restaurant for mosquitoes, flies, and gnats, which is not very pleasant for him." Judy gave Starlight a pat and smiled at her audience. "Think of it. How would you like to spend your entire summer being bitten by bugs with nothing but your tail to protect you?"

"Ugh!" everyone groaned together.

Judy smiled again. "Okay. Now you see why horses depend on us to protect them from insects, and with Starlight's help here, I'm going to demonstrate exactly how to do it."

Starlight watched with interest as Judy picked up a plastic bottle and sprayed insect repellent on his lower legs. She talked as she worked.

"When you spray your horse like this, start with its legs, so it won't be frightened. Then move slowly up its body, but never squirt anything in its face. That's dangerous to its eyes and will scare it."

She put the spray bottle down and picked up what looked like a bottle of roll-on deodorant. "For their faces, you can use products like this." She rolled the liquid around Starlight's eyes and mouth. Starlight wrinkled up his nose, as if the insecticide smelled funny.

"If the horseflies really get bad this summer, you can use these." Judy held up a horse blanket made of thin, meshy material that was designed to keep flies away. "Or, if horseflies just buzz around your horse's eyes, you can use one of these ear nets."

She picked up something that looked like a purple sock with two big toes. Carole held Starlight while Judy pulled the thing snug over the top of his head. His ears suddenly became two purple points. A fringe of little purple tassels hung down in front of his eyes. When Carole turned Starlight to face the audience, everyone began to roar with laughter.

"He looks like he's got one of my grandmother's lamp shades on his head!" a boy howled from the back row.

That made everyone laugh even harder. Even Max was chortling. When Carole and Judy turned to look at Starlight themselves, Carole started to giggle; then Judy joined in. "It's true." Carole laughed, and tears came to her eyes. "Starlight does look like he's wearing a lamp shade!"

"Well, this contraption may look a little unusual," Judy said when the laughter finally subsided. "But I guarantee your horse would rather look like a lamp shade than be made miserable all summer by flies." She grinned and rubbed Starlight's neck as she removed the ear net. "Are there any questions?"

Nobody had any, so she gave the lead line back to Carole.

"Then let's have a big hand for Starlight for being so patient and for his owner, Carole Hanson."

Everyone cheered and clapped. Starlight seemed to know he'd pleased the crowd. He switched his tail and pranced a little as Carole led him back to the barn.

"You are such a wonderful horse," she said, giving him a kiss on the nose as she hurriedly put him back in his stall. "Even if you did look like a big lamp with that thing on your head, you didn't misbehave once!"

She ran back out and joined Stevie and Lisa. Judy was just finishing up her lecture.

"With regular tube worming and spraying and even our little lamp-shade hats, we can keep these horses healthy and comfortable all summer long."

Everyone stood up and clapped as Judy ended her talk. She shook Max's hand again and carried her supplies to her truck.

"Okay," Max said. "Everybody go tack up and bring your mounts back out here to the ring. We're going to divide into teams and play some games."

"How many teams?" someone asked.

"Two. Divide up by the first letter of your last name. A through M versus N through Z."

The group raced toward the stables. Lisa and Carole and Stevie hurried along behind the younger riders.

"I thought I was going to die when Judy put that ear net on Starlight's head," Stevie said, still chuckling.

Carole laughed. "I know. It was hysterical! But he didn't seem to mind. In fact, I think he enjoyed it."

"He was the star of the show," said Lisa. "Starlight has real stage presence!"

"I'm so glad I worked all those kinks out of him," Carole said. "I don't know what he would have done if Judy had tried to put that fly hat on him a week ago."

They tacked up and met the rest of Horse Wise by the outdoor ring. Just to be sure that Starlight wouldn't act up, Carole decided to run him for a little while before they joined the games. She didn't want a repeat performance of their last riding class, particularly after Starlight had been the hit of Horse Wise.

"I'll catch up with you two later," Carole said to Stevie and Lisa as she led Starlight toward the big paddock. "I'm going to give Starlight one more dose of my antikink medicine, just to be sure."

"But he was so good with Judy and the fly hat," said Lisa.

"I know," replied Carole. "But better safe than sorry." She tugged Starlight's bridle to keep him from sidling over into Belle.

"Don't be too long," Stevie called. "We need you on our team. We don't want to be beaten by the last half of the alphabet!"

Stevie and Lisa continued toward the ring while Carole led Starlight to the upper end of the paddock and climbed aboard.

As usual, Starlight was fidgety at first, backing up instead of going forward, then going sideways. Carole made him stop and collect himself; then she urged him into a brisk trot. Just as before, the more he moved, the better he behaved. They had covered half the paddock at a trot when she gave him the signal to canter.

The big bay horse moved seamlessly into the easy, three-beat gait that felt to Carole as comfortable as sitting in a rocking chair. His ears flicked forward, and he seemed to enjoy the freedom of stretching his legs in the green pasture. Halfway down the long field, Carole sat forward in her seat slightly, touched him behind the girth with her right heel, and loosened the reins. Starlight recognized the signals, and *zoom!* they were off at a gallop. Birds scattered from the underbrush as Carole and Starlight zipped through the tall grass.

They galloped the length of the paddock. Then Carole pulled him down into a trot. He obeyed instantly. After every gallop he was again the willing, dependable horse she loved.

"Good boy!" she said, patting his neck. "Now that you're acting like your old self, we need to get back and help out the girls."

Starlight tossed his head as he trotted back toward the riding ring, eager to return to the other horses and do his part in the games.

By the time Carole and Starlight reentered the ring, the teams were tied. The last event, the tennis racket relay, was almost finished.

"Over here, Carole!" Stevie frantically waved her arms. "Take my place! You and Starlight are better at this than Belle and I, and our team only needs one point to win!"

Carole trotted over to Stevie. "Are you sure?" she asked. She knew how much Stevie loved to compete and didn't want to take her turn away from her.

"Sure I'm sure," said Stevie.

Stevie and Belle moved out of line while Carole and Starlight took their place. Lisa and Prancer were just twisting through the last section of the poles. Lisa held a tennis racket in her left hand with a ball balanced on the face of it. At the last pole, the ball careened perilously to one edge of the racket, but Lisa recovered just in time and passed it to Carole with a gasp.

"There!" she cried. "Go!"

Carole and Starlight took off. They had to curve tightly through a series of poles, keeping the ball balanced on the racket strings. She and Starlight had a slight lead, but out of the corner of her eye she could see Joe Novick catching up fast on his big gray gelding.

"Hurry, Starlight!" Carole whispered as they turned the end pole and began twisting their way back to the finish line. She crouched low over Starlight's shoulders as she guided him through the curving course. The tennis ball bounced once, and for a moment she thought she'd dropped it, but it landed back in the middle of the racket and stayed there. The last ten yards of the course were straight.

"Go, Starlight, go!" she cried as they rounded the last pole.

Starlight leaped into a canter. Carole held on to him with her legs and the tennis racket with her hand. With a thunder of hooves, she and Starlight crossed the finish line an instant before Joe Novick. A loud cheer went up from her team. Carole leaned over in the saddle and gave Starlight a big hug. Thanks to him, their team had won by a nose!

"All *right!*" Stevie said as she and Lisa rode over. The three girls lifted their hands together in a high fifteen. "We knew you could do it!"

"Thanks." Carole smiled down at Starlight. He had been the hit of the day—first by modeling the fly hat, then by winning the relay race for their team. And he'd been a cooperative and well-mannered horse the whole time. She felt a warm glow of pride as she gave his neck a rub. She had known all along what was wrong with Starlight, and she had known exactly what to do about it. Not every horse owner in the world could say that!

STEVIE COLLAPSED ON the bench in front of her cubby. "That was one of the best Horse Wise meetings ever!"

"I know," Lisa agreed as she pulled off her tall black boots. "Carole, you and Starlight really saved the day."

"Thanks." Carole smiled with satisfaction. It had been a good day. She had finally worked Starlight through all his difficulties, and they had had a good time doing it. She loosened her dark hair from its braid and let it fall to her shoulders. "Hey, are we still going shopping for Jamie this afternoon?"

"I think so," said Lisa. "Can anybody's mom or dad take us to the mall?"

"Mine can't," grumbled Stevie. "They're poring over their law books. They've both got big cases in court next week."

"My dad's reviewing a dress parade even as we speak," Carole said. "How about your mom, Lisa?"

"No, she had to go and see the decorator about getting the living room redone." Lisa shook her head. "I can't wait to see how that will turn out!"

"I guess we'll have to walk to the shopping center where TD's is, then," said Stevie. "Maybe that little gift shop will have something Jamie would like."

They walked over to TD's but for once passed by the ice cream shop. "I wonder if our favorite waitress is there?" Stevie cupped her hands around her eyes and peered through the front window.

Carole laughed. "She probably thinks that last ice cream concoction you ordered killed you and she's hiding out from the police."

"It didn't kill me in the least." Stevie patted her stomach. "In fact, it restored me to health."

The girls trooped past the supermarket and the electronics store and turned into the small gift shop. Just inside the door stood a circular case filled with small crystal animals. Dolphins and dragons and unicorns glittered like diamonds on the black velvet shelves.

"Look!" said Lisa. "Aren't these beautiful?"

Stevie and Carole crowded around her. "They're gorgeous," said Stevie. "But I don't think a six-year-old boy would get much of a charge out of them." She turned toward another part of the store.

Carole was about to follow her when a strangely famil-

103

iar shape caught her eye. "Wait!" she cried. "There's Pegasus!"

The girls peered at the figurines again. Sure enough, at the very back was a small crystal horse rearing on its hind legs, just about to spread its wings and fly.

"Isn't he fantastic?" Carole said.

Lisa nodded. "He's beautiful!"

Carole looked at the price tag attached to Pegasus. Though he was expensive, he was on sale, and she had just enough money to buy him and still contribute to Jamie's gift. She knew it would wreck her budget, but maybe she could do some extra chores around the house for her dad to make up the difference. Pegasus was worth it. Creatures that beautiful didn't come along very often.

"I'm going to buy him," Carole announced decisively. "I'm going to take him home and look at him every day. That way I'll be inspired when the time comes to do my project." She dug in her purse for her wallet. "Why don't you two go look for a gift for Jamie while I pay for Pegasus. That way we can save some time."

"Okay," Stevie agreed. She and Lisa sauntered off to browse through the gift shop while Carole paid for Pegasus. By the time the clerk had wrapped him securely in bubble wrap and given Carole her change, Stevie and Lisa reappeared, their faces flat with disappointment.

"We've looked at everything they have." Lisa sounded frustrated. "And it's either too babyish or too grown up."

"Unless Jamie would like some rose-scented potpourri,"

104

griped Stevie. "There's just not much here for a six-year-old with chicken pox."

"What shall we do?" Carole asked as she put Pegasus safely inside her purse.

"Maybe we could just go over to Jamie's house for a visit," suggested Lisa. "Since we've all had chicken pox, we could talk to him and maybe help cheer him up."

"That's a good idea," said Stevie.

"Fine with me." Carole happily patted her purse.

The Bacons' house was not far away. The girls crossed the street in front of TD's, then turned down a little side street that curved along a small creek. Soon they were standing on Jamie's front porch, ringing the doorbell.

For a long moment no one answered. Then Mrs. Bacon opened the door.

"Why, Lisa, Stevie, Carole! What a surprise!" She smiled, but there were deep lines of fatigue around her mouth, and her face looked pale and tired. The girls had seen the same signs on Max and Deborah, and they knew exactly what had caused them—a small child with chicken pox.

"Hi, Mrs. Bacon." Lisa spoke for the group. "We finished with our Horse Wise class and wondered if we might come over and say hello to Jamie. You know, to try to cheer him up."

"Well, how nice of you girls. Please come in." Mrs. Bacon held the door open. Her normally spotless living room was cluttered with the morning paper, a half-empty cup of coffee, and a scattering of Jamie's crayons and coloring books.

"I'm sorry the house is such a wreck. It seems like I spend all my nights trying to keep Jamie comfortable and all my days trying to keep him entertained. I'm afraid I'm way behind on my housekeeping, and I don't know when I'm going to catch up."

"That sounds a lot like what our friends went through when their baby girl had chicken pox," Lisa said.

"Well, it's not that chicken pox is all that dangerous. As childhood diseases go, it's usually not serious at all. But it just makes whoever has it so cranky. It breaks my heart to see Jamie lying in there so itchy and miserable." Mrs. Bacon gave a heavy sigh. "Now he's awake from his nap and I'm so tired I can barely keep my eyes open."

"Why don't you go and rest for a couple of hours and let us take care of Jamie?" Stevie said. "Lisa can read him a story and Carole can play charades with him and I can teach him all my good jokes. We came over here to cheer him up, anyway. Now we can cheer him up and let you get some rest at the same time."

Mrs. Bacon blinked. "Would you girls really be willing to do that?"

"Sure!" Lisa and Carole said together.

"Well, I'm certainly not going to turn down such a wonderful offer." Mrs. Bacon smiled in gratitude. "Let's see . . . Lisa, you know where things are in the kitchen, and where the telephone is if someone calls." She shrugged her shoulders and grinned. "You've got a deal!"

Mrs. Bacon turned to lead them down the hall, then stopped. "Oh, just one thing," she said. "All of you have had chicken pox, haven't you?"

"Oh, yes," the girls reassured her. "We all had it years ago."

"Perfect," Mrs. Bacon said. "Then follow me." She led them to Jamie's room and tapped softly on the door.

"Come in," a small, woeful voice responded.

"Hi, Jamie." Mrs. Bacon peeked in the room. "I've got a surprise for you. Look who's here!"

She opened the door wider to reveal Carole, Lisa, and Stevie standing there. "Hi, Jamie!" they greeted the sick little boy.

"I'll leave all of you to have a nice visit," Mrs. Bacon whispered, hurrying down the hall to her own room. "See you in a couple of hours!"

"Hi, everybody." Jamie smiled as the girls sat down on the foot of his bed. His face and neck were covered in red, blotchy pox.

"How are you feeling?" Lisa asked softly. "We haven't seen you since Wednesday."

"Pretty itchy," he replied with a sigh. "But I haven't thrown up anymore."

"That's good," said Carole. "As I remember, we ate some pretty weird stuff Wednesday."

"Yeah." Jamie smiled. "But it sure tasted good. And the rides were great. Did they ever fix the merry-go-round?"

"Nope," Stevie reported. "I was there until late Wednesday night, and the merry-go-round hadn't turned an inch. You didn't miss a thing."

"Gosh, Jamie, you've got some neat books over here." Lisa bent over and looked at the books beside his bed. "Would you like us to read you one?"

Jamie nodded.

"Let's see." Lisa ran her finger along the titles. "How about *Where the Wild Things Are?*"

"Okay."

Lisa plumped up Jamie's pillows and sat beside him to read. Carole and Stevie relaxed on the end of the bed, listening as Lisa read the words and Jamie studied the pictures. When Lisa finished, he looked up and smiled.

"That's one of my favorite stories," he said softly. "Sometimes at night I think there are wild things under my bed."

"Shall I check for you, just to be sure?" Stevie asked, leaning upside down over the bed till her head touched the floor. She lifted up the bed skirt and peeked underneath. "Nothing wild down here," she reported. "But look what I found!" She held up a game of Candy Land. "Want to play?"

"Sure," Jamie said.

Lisa put a pillow on Jamie's lap, and Stevie set up the game. Stevie and Jamie played while Lisa and Carole watched. Around and around the board they went, until Jamie finally won.

"Yay!" he said. Again his voice was soft.

"Want to play again?" asked Stevie. "And let me avenge my honor?"

Jamie shook his head. "I don't think so."

"Want to read another book?" Lisa asked.

"No thanks."

"Want me to show you how to make an origami goldfish?" Carole offered.

"No thanks," Jamie replied again, beginning to scratch at a chicken pox on his neck.

"Then what would you like to do, Jamie?" Lisa asked.

"I don't know." Jamie sighed. "Sometimes I run out of fun stuff to do."

"Would you like me to tell you a story, Jamie?" Carole sat up and looked at him, her dark brown eyes bright. "A story about a wonderful, magical horse that could fly?"

"You mean the one you were reading about at the stable?" Jamie asked, suddenly smiling.

"That's the one. Just lie back on your pillows and listen."

Everyone settled down on the bed and listened as Carole told the legend of Pegasus and Bellerophon. She told of King Iobates, the Chimera, the Amazons, and finally Pegasus' gift of immortality from Zeus. When she finished, Jamie clapped his hands.

"That's the neatest story I've ever heard!" he cried.

"Then let me show you something else," Carole said. She dug in her purse and pulled out the thick bundle of bubble wrap. Slowly she unwrapped it and placed the crystal Pegasus right on Jamie's lap.

"Wow!" he breathed, stroking Pegasus' wings with one finger. "That's a whole lot neater than the pony on the merry-go-round!"

Suddenly Carole realized that today Pegasus was far more important to Jamie than he was to her. Jamie needed Pegasus to feel better right now, while she only needed Pegasus for inspiration on a school project that wasn't due for three months.

"Tell you what, Jamie," she said with a smile. "I bought Pegasus for me, but why don't I lend him to you to help you feel better? You can keep him until your last chicken pox is gone, and then you can give him back."

"Gosh." Jamie's eyes grew wide. "Thanks! I'll take good care of him."

Just then the door opened. Mrs. Bacon stood there. The tired lines on her face had magically disappeared, and her pretty blue eyes looked bright again.

"How's everybody doing in here? I can't believe I've been asleep for almost two hours!"

"We've been having a great time!" Jamie said excitedly, cupping Pegasus in his hand.

"Well, Jamie, I think we need to let these girls get home now. Why don't you say good-bye? And maybe they can come back some other time."

"Okay." Jamie grinned up at Lisa, Stevie, and Carole. "Bye," he said. "Thanks for coming by and playing with me."

"We enjoyed it, Jamie," Lisa replied. "You just concentrate on getting better."

Carole waved and Stevie gave him a wink. They followed Mrs. Bacon back out into the living room.

"I really can't thank you girls enough," she said. "I feel like a new person. It's amazing what two hours of sleep will do." She reached for her purse. "Lisa, I want to pay you what I owe you for baby-sitting the first half of this week, and since you were so nice to drop by today, I'll pay you what you would have earned Thursday and Friday."

"Oh, thank you, Mrs. Bacon." Lisa was so happy she leaned over and gave Mrs. Bacon a hug. With this money, she now had the fifty dollars she'd promised her parents. Her riding lessons would not end!

Mrs. Bacon gave a little laugh. "Gosh, Lisa, I had no idea you were this interested in baby-sitting. Would you like to come some more next week?"

"Oh, absolutely!" Lisa said. She realized it would be a perfect trade-off for her—the more she baby-sat, the more she could ride. "I could even come tomorrow afternoon if you'd like to take another nice long nap."

"Actually, I'm hoping Jamie will sleep well enough tonight so that I won't need a nap tomorrow, but it would be wonderful if you could come by Monday afternoon."

"Sure," agreed Lisa.

Mrs. Bacon frowned quizzically at the girls. "Say, I want to ask you something. What exactly happened Wednesday at the fair? I know Jamie came home cranky and sick, but ever since then all he's talked about is what a wonderful time he had. What did you three do?"

Lisa smiled, pleased that Jamie had enjoyed himself in spite of being sick. "Well, we thought he was really upset about the merry-go-round being broken, so we tried everything we knew to distract him from that and make him feel good. You know, lots of rides, games, candy and popcorn and stuff."

Mrs. Bacon laughed. "Oh, so it was good old-fashioned bribery!"

"Well, sort of, I guess," Lisa said, embarrassed that Mrs. Bacon had caught on to their tactic so fast.

"Listen, Jamie's dad and I have often resorted to the old bribe routine ourselves," Mrs. Bacon said, chuckling. "The trouble is, it rarely works. The only thing we've found that really helps is getting down to the root of the problem, which, in this instance, was a case of chicken pox."

"You know, that reminds me of a problem I was having with my horse," Carole began.

Stevie and Lisa looked at each other and sighed. Only Carole Hanson could find a connection between a horse with a star on his forehead and a six-year-old with chicken pox on his face.

"Starlight has been misbehaving because he's been shut up all winter, so I have to let him run around, and—"

"Wait a minute, Carole," Lisa said with a frown. "Starlight hasn't been shut up all winter. He's been indoors, but you've ridden him nearly every day, just like you're doing now."

"But—"

"Lisa's right, Carole," added Stevie. "You must have forgotten how much you've ridden him."

"But why does he still misbehave?" Carole asked, holding her hands out helplessly.

"Maybe he's got chicken pox, too," Mrs. Bacon said, laughing.

Everyone chuckled, but the words stuck in Carole's mind. Chicken pox had made Jamie itchy and *cranky*. If Starlight had been anything lately, it was cranky. Though Carole knew it wasn't possible for Starlight to have chicken pox, she suddenly had a sick feeling in her stomach. All at once she realized that she'd been treating Starlight for what *she* thought was wrong with him. She'd never actually looked at him to find out what else, if anything, might be the matter.

"Excuse me," she said, interrupting a conversation Mrs. Bacon was having with Stevie. "But I've got to go and see about my horse. I think I may have been overlooking something really important!"

With that, she turned and let herself out the door. Lisa, Stevie, and Mrs. Bacon watched in amazement as Carole ran down the street and turned in the direction of Pine Hollow.

"Gosh," said Mrs. Bacon with concern. "She seemed upset. I hope she didn't take my remark about chicken pox seriously."

Lisa and Stevie smiled. "Don't worry about it, Mrs. Bacon," said Lisa. "That's just Carole. With her, horses always come first."

CAROLE HURRIED ALONG the road to Pine Hollow. As her footsteps echoed on the pavement, she thought about all the things Starlight might have been trying to tell her that she had been too busy to understand.

"I thought I knew just what was right for him," she whispered. "And all along I was just bribing him to behave. It's just like Jamie at the fair. I haven't been treating what was wrong with him."

Quickly she turned off the road and into the parking lot. Though the late afternoon was still sunny, all the day's riding lessons were finished, and only Max's car was still parked there. The stable itself looked empty, with no riders leading horses in or out. When she walked inside, all she heard was the steady crunch of stabled horses eating oats. She scurried down one aisle, turned past Chip and Patch and Barq, and opened the door to Starlight's stall. Starlight was leaning to the right, trying to rub his neck against the stable wall.

"Oh, Starlight!" she cried. "I owe you a huge apology!"

The big bay stared at her, his ears pricked.

Carole looked into Starlight's eyes. "Starlight, I haven't been treating you as a friend deserves to be treated. I've ignored the things you've tried to tell me, and I've been dreaming about imaginary horses when I should have been paying attention to the real horse that loves me. I am so sorry for doing that. When I get home I'm going to put Pegasus on my bookshelf. Then I'm going to give you every ounce of my attention so that you can be the healthiest horse in the world."

Starlight nickered softly and stamped his front foot, as if he agreed with what she said.

Carole smiled. "Don't move, Starlight," she said. "I'll be right back."

She ran to the tack room, got her grooming supplies, and hurried back to her horse. "We're going to start with the basics," she told him as she led him out of his stall and attached him to the cross-ties. "I'm going to check you out from A to Z."

Though she knew she did not have a vet's training or experience, she did the same examination on Starlight that she'd watched Judy do on the Albergini horses. She checked his teeth, eyes, and ears, then felt along his legs and spine. Everything seemed normal. "I think all your body parts are okay, Starlight," she said, relieved that she had not overlooked some serious leg or back inflammation in her mistaken diagnosis of the winter kinks.

He watched with curiosity as she felt along his belly for infected mosquito bites, but there were no telltale bumps around his girth line. She looked under his tail and between his back legs for ticks, but again, his skin was smooth, with no engorged insects attached.

"That leaves just one more thing," she said.

She ran to the bathroom and pulled a paper towel from the dispenser. Then she came back to Starlight and ran the currycomb gently under his jaw, catching all the dirt and dander on the towel. She took it over to the window and held it flat in the afternoon light so that she could examine it more closely. There, wiggling on the towel, was what she had feared: lice. Starlight was infested with lice.

For a moment she just stared numbly at the tiny, disgusting bugs crawling around on the paper towel. How could she have missed this? She had been on a vet call with Judy where she'd diagnosed a horse with lice. She'd known about them for years from her horse books. She'd even held Starlight in a demonstration about how to prevent bug infestation. And he had been sick with lice the whole time!

Carole felt her face grow hot with shame and anger. "You were so absolutely positive you knew exactly what was wrong with him you never once considered anything else," she told herself sternly. "Some horse owner you are."

She wadded up the paper towel and threw it in the garbage can. Then she walked back to where Starlight was cross-tied.

"I am so sorry, Starlight," she said. "I owe you a hug, but not till you're clean. I promise that I will never, ever let anything like this happen to you again!" She smiled up at him. "Get ready for the grooming of your life!"

She covered the ground where Starlight stood with old newspapers. Then she curried and brushed him until his coat was free of dust and dirt. After carefully combing through his mane and tail, she went to the tack room and mixed up a large bucket of the insecticide solution Judy had recommended at the demonstration.

"Okay," she said as she lugged the full bucket back out to Starlight. "Here comes the fun part."

She put on rubber gloves and soaked a sponge in the insecticide solution. Then, slowly and carefully, she doused Starlight in the stinky stuff, making sure it soaked through his hair right down to his skin. Starlight stood still for the process, but when Carole finished up at his tail, he looked around as if wondering when she was going to rinse everything off.

"Not now, Starlight," she said, laughing at his puzzled expression. "We have to let this dry. Then we have to do it all over again in two weeks."

Starlight blinked unbelievingly, and Carole laughed again. "But why don't I let you drip dry out in the paddock while I clean your stall? That would be a lot nicer for you."

117

She let him loose in the small paddock by the barn and returned to his stall. There she forked up every bit of his old bedding, sprinkled lime on the floor, dusted it with lice powder, and put down a thick layer of fresh sawdust. Barq poked his head around from the next stall and watched her as she worked.

"What are you looking at, Barq?" Carole laughed as his round Arabian eyes followed her every move. "You're going to get exactly the same treatment as soon as I finish here." Carole knew that it was very likely that Barq and Belle, who lived on either side of Starlight, were infested with lice, too. She also knew that as a responsible horse owner, it was her duty to take care of them as well.

She finished with Starlight's stall and began the same lice treatment on Barq.

An hour later, when Barq and his stall were both lice-free, she started on Belle. She was halfway through soaking her with the insecticide solution when she heard footsteps down the hall.

"Pheewww!" she heard Max exclaim. "Who's got the lice dip out?"

Carole looked down the hall. Suddenly Max appeared.

"Oh, Max," Carole cried, "I was all wrong about Starlight! He didn't have the winter kinks! He had lice!"

"Oh?" Max walked up and patted Belle on the rump. "What makes you think that?"

Carole knelt down. The hair of the three horses she'd groomed was intermingled on the newspaper—a mahogany-dark brown combination of Starlight, Belle, and Barq. Carole picked up some of Starlight's hair and held it up to Max. "Look. You can still see the bugs crawling around."

Max frowned at Starlight's hair sample, then picked up some from Barq and Belle. "They're in Barq's, too," he said, squinting at the tiny, crawling bugs. He dropped the hair back on the newspaper and looked at Carole. "What made you think of this? I thought you were certain that he just had too much energy from not being ridden enough."

"I was," Carole replied. "But he never got any better, however much I rode him. Then Lisa reminded me that I'd never *not* ridden him, really. I rode almost every day during the school year." She sighed. "It suddenly hit me that I hadn't been treating him as much as bribing him, so I came back here and gave him a physical, just like I'd seen Judy do. When I checked under his jaws I found what had really been the matter with him. Lice. Barq and Belle had them too. Thank goodness Belle didn't have them badly. I couldn't have faced Stevie."

Max looked at Belle thoughtfully. "Stevie would have understood, but I should have suspected that right away," he said. "By nature Starlight's not a temperamental animal. I should have known something like this was going on, but you seemed to know exactly what was wrong with him." He smiled at Carole. "This reminds me of a set of parents who were certain their baby girl was just being fussy, when she happened to be coming down with a case of chicken pox!"

Carole laughed. "There seems to be a lot of that going around—chicken pox *and* certainty!"

Max gave Belle another pat. "I'll tell Red that we'll need to spray the whole barn. Have you cleaned out these horses' stalls?"

"I've done Starlight's and Barq's. I'll do Belle's as soon as I finish dousing her with insecticide."

Max nodded. "Okay. When you're done with Belle, bring all this hair and newspaper out to the trash pile. We'll need to burn it. I'll go around and take a lice count on everybody else."

Carole watched as Max went into Patch's stall. Checking as expertly as Judy Barker had done, he felt beneath Patch's jaws, at the base of his tail, and along his neck and flanks. "Good news," Max reported as Patch nickered. "Nobody home. At least no lice, anyway."

Carole breathed a sigh of relief. She would never have forgiven herself if every horse in the stable had been full of lice because of her negligence with Starlight. *Maybe not too many others will be infested,* she thought as she watched Max begin to work his way down the stalls.

It was dark by the time they finished. Though Max only found one or two lice on Calypso and Romeo, Carole gave them and their stalls the whole treatment. By the time she had finished, her arms and legs ached as they never had before. Wearily she hauled all the newspaper out to the small fire pit that was a hundred yards away from the stable.

"Is that all of it?" Max asked, pulling a water hose close to the pit.

"Yes," said Carole, out of breath as she dumped the last of the newspapers. "That's everything—horse hair, dander, dead and living lice."

"Good," Max said. "This shouldn't take long."

He lit a match and tossed it under the pile of newspaper. For a moment nothing happened; then orange flames began to lick around the edges of the paper. In an instant the whole pile was a small ball of flame. Then, as quickly as it had ignited, it went out. The only thing left was black, sooty ashes. Nonetheless, Max turned the hose on and drenched the pit with water. "You can never be too careful with fire around a barn," he said, reaching down and feeling the ashes to make sure they were totally cold and thoroughly soaked.

"And you can't be too careful with parasites, either," Carole said. "I'm so glad none of the other horses was suffering as much as Starlight was." She shook her head. "But I'm so sorry he had to suffer at all. He never will again." She looked at Max and took a vow. "If I have anything to do with it, none of the horses here will ever suffer from lice or ticks or horseflies again."

Max smiled and began to coil up the hose. "I think it's great that you feel that way, Carole. But you've also got to be realistic."

"What do you mean?" Carole frowned.

"I mean that we can't kill every bug or fly that lands on a

121

horse. It would be impossible. Botflies and lice and ticks are just part of the total package. For all the good, wonderful things that come with horses, a few bad things come along, too. It's part of owning a horse."

He stashed the hose underneath a tree. "The trick is to be aware of what exactly is going on with your horse. Realize that parasites might be bothering him when he gets cranky, and take care of them before they get out of hand. Horses can't ask for a dose of insecticide. And they certainly can't suit themselves up with an ear net before they go out for a run in the paddock."

Carole giggled at the thought of Starlight tucking his ears up in one of those lamp shade–looking hats, but she knew Max was making a serious point. Suddenly she wanted to see Starlight and apologize all over again.

"I'm going to put Starlight back in his stall," she said, leaving Max and hurrying back to the barn. As soon as she closed the stall door, Starlight began munching his hay. Though he smelled like insecticide, his eyes were bright, and he greeted her with his old soft nicker as he looked up from his food.

"Hey, Starlight," Carole said, rubbing him behind his ears. She looked into his big brown eyes and smiled. "I'm sorry I didn't listen to what you were trying to tell me. From now on, even though I may not be able to figure it out right off the bat, I'm going to listen to you first and try out my own crazy theories later!"

Starlight blinked unconcernedly, then went back to munching his hay.

"I think he's forgiven you, Carole," Max said, coming up behind her. "Now I think you'd better forgive yourself."

Carole smiled. As usual, Max had guessed her feelings.

"Say, how about we call it a night and I'll give you a lift home? Does your dad know where you are?"

"Yes, I called him this afternoon to tell him I'd probably be here till late."

"Well, I'm sure he wouldn't want you taking the bus this time of night."

"Thanks, Max," Carole said, feeling almost limp with fatigue. "That would be great."

They shut the stable door and walked to the parking lot. Carole buckled her seat belt as they pulled out of the driveway; then she leaned back against the headrest. She was asleep before Max's car was out of the driveway.

"WHEN IS LISA supposed to get here with Jamie?" Stevie asked impatiently, rearranging herself on the bale of hay.

Carole didn't look up from her book. "When her mother finishes meeting with the decorator, she's going to give Lisa and Jamie a ride over here."

"It seems like it's taken him forever to get well." Stevie drew her knees up under her chin and stared out into the parking lot.

"We visited him just over a week ago, Stevie," Carole reminded her. "That's the normal recovery time for chicken pox."

Stevie sighed and frowned. "I thought you'd given up reading at the stable. You said it distracted you from Starlight."

Carole held up her book. On the cover was a picture of a

124

kind-looking man with a beautiful Thoroughbred peeking out from behind his shoulder. Just over that were the title and author: *The Man Who Listens to Horses* by Monty Roberts. Carole smiled. "This won't distract me from Starlight. This will help me figure out what he's trying to tell me."

"I know what Starlight's trying to tell you," Stevie announced.

"What?"

" 'Ride me, Carole, ride me.' " Stevie bugged out her eyes and spoke in a hypnotic voice. " 'It's summer vacation . . . no time for reading. . . . Put the book down and ride me!' "

Suddenly a car horn tooted.

"Look!" Stevie leaped to her feet. "There's Lisa now."

The green sedan pulled to a stop. Both doors on the passenger side opened. "Hi, everybody!" Jamie cried, getting out of the backseat.

"Hi, Jamie!" Stevie and Carole called as Jamie ran toward them. Lisa followed, but more slowly.

"Hey, how are you feeling?" Carole asked as the little boy ran up and threw his arms around her waist.

"I'm feeling great!"

"Are all your chicken pox gone?" Stevie asked as she also received a hug.

"All but one," Jamie reported proudly. He lifted up his shirt to reveal the last remaining spot on his stomach. "It's almost gone," he said. "And it doesn't itch at all."

"Hi, guys." Lisa greeted them with a smile. "As you can see, Jamie's feeling much better."

"He looks terrific," Carole said. "Rosy cheeks, bright eyes, lots of energy."

"I'll give you three guesses what the first thing he wanted to do when he got better was."

"Let's see . . . ," Stevie said, shooting Carole a teasing glance. "Did you want to read a book?"

"No," Jamie said.

"Did you want to eat candy and junk food until you felt like you might throw up?" Stevie guessed again.

"No." Jamie laughed and shook his head.

"Hmmm." Stevie frowned and chewed her fingernail, pretending to be stumped. "Could it be . . . Did you want to visit your Saddle Club pals and ride Nickel?"

"Yes!" Jamie cried.

"All right!" said Carole. "I knew we'd made a believer out of him!"

"Do you think Max would mind?" Lisa asked. "Mrs. Bacon says it's all he's talked about for the past two weeks."

"Why don't you three go visit Nickel in his stall, and I'll go ask Max for permission," Stevie volunteered. "I'm sure he'll say yes, though. Anybody who recovers from chicken pox is a hero in his book."

Carole and Lisa took Jamie into the stable to visit Nickel, while Stevie went to look for Max. In a few minutes she returned, smiling. "He said it's fine with him, as long as we use a helmet and spot him."

"Then let's go," said Lisa. They led Nickel out of his stall and clipped him to the cross-ties. Carole taught Jamie how to use a currycomb, and Stevie demonstrated the fundamentals of hoof picking. Lisa brought Nickel's saddle and bridle from the tack room, and in a few minutes he was ready to go.

"Wow," Jamie said as he buckled on the black helmet. "Learning all this real stuff is a lot better than riding a merry-go-round!"

"That's exactly the way we feel, Jamie," Carole said.

Jamie touched the Pine Hollow horseshoe for luck, and together they led Nickel out to the riding ring.

"Remember how to mount up?" Carole asked.

"Of course he does," Stevie snorted. "He did it just fine two weeks ago."

Lisa gave him a boost, and Jamie mounted Nickel perfectly. With Stevie and Carole spotting on either side, Lisa began to lead Nickel around the ring.

"Is it as fun as you remembered?" she asked over her shoulder.

Jamie nodded vigorously. "It's great! Can we go faster now?"

"Carole? Stevie?" Lisa asked. "Ready to trot?"

"I suppose," Stevie replied. "But not too long. It's really hot out here."

They trotted around the ring three times, then stopped back at the gate. "Thanks," said Jamie, his face pink with excitement. "That was great."

"You'll have to come back and do it again," Lisa said. "Someday when Stevie is in better shape."

"Ha, ha," grumbled Stevie.

THE SADDLE CLUB

Jamie dismounted, and they led Nickel back to the barn. "Hey, Carole," he said. "Wait. I've got something to give you."

They stopped while Jamie ran to the backpack he'd left beside the stable door. He dug down deep inside it and pulled out a bundle wrapped up in a small plastic bag. He smiled as he handed it to Carole.

She knew what it was the moment she touched it. She looked at Jamie. "This is Pegasus, isn't it?"

He nodded. "He helped me get better. When I lay in bed all itchy, I would look at him and remember Nickel and think of how much fun it was going to be when I could come back here and ride." Jamie smiled. "Now he can help you with your project."

As Carole held the bag in her hands, she could feel the outline of Pegasus' legs and outstretched wings. Suddenly she knew she'd done the right thing by loaning him to Jamie. It wasn't really a bribe. Pegasus had just reminded Jamie that his chicken pox wouldn't last forever and that happier, healthier days would soon come.

"Thanks for remembering to give him back, Jamie. I really appreciate it," Carole said. "And you're right. He can help me with my project. Maybe when I look at him, my words will soar!"

"Oh, brother." Stevie rolled her eyes.

Suddenly, Lisa realized it was time for her to take Jamie home. Mrs. Bacon hadn't wanted him to get overly tired.

128

"Gosh, Jamie." Lisa looked at her watch. "We're going to be late."

"Go ahead and walk him home, Lisa," Carole suggested. "Stevie and I will take care of Nickel. Why don't you just plan on meeting us at TD's in half an hour?"

"Okay. Thanks. You guys are lifesavers."

Jamie said good-bye to everybody. Lisa took him by the hand, and they hurried on toward his house. Carole and Stevie walked Nickel back to his stall.

"Do you want to do the tack or Nickel?" Carole asked as she unbuckled the pony's bridle and slipped a halter on him.

"I don't know." Stevie shrugged. "I don't care."

"Well, why don't you put his tack back and I'll brush him down?" Carole suggested pleasantly.

"Whatever," snapped Stevie, loosening Nickel's girth.

Carole looked at her friend. "Stevie, why are you so grouchy today?"

"Have I been grouchy?" Stevie's eyes widened in surprise.

"A little bit," Carole replied as she began currying Nickel's soft coat.

"I'm sorry," Stevie said earnestly. "I didn't realize that I had been."

"It's okay," said Carole. "Just as long as nothing is wrong."

Fifteen minutes later Nickel was brushed and happily munching hay in his stall. His tack had been cleaned and put in its proper place, and Stevie and Carole stood in front of their horses' stalls.

"Hey, boy." Carole gave Starlight his usual rub behind the ears, but today she added a scratch under his jaw and along his mane. He seemed to enjoy it, and it was a good way for her to make absolutely sure he was free of lice. He still smelled of insecticide, but he was no longer trying to scratch his neck against the stall walls, and he was his old regular self under the saddle again.

"I'm going to TD's with Stevie and Lisa, then I'm coming back and we're going for a ride," Carole told him. He pricked his ears, listening. "Then after that, I'll give you a good grooming and get all the tangles out of your tail."

"Are you ready to go?" Stevie suddenly appeared behind Carole, again looking at her watch.

"Yes, I was just talking to Starlight—"

"Well, we need to hurry. It's already almost one."

"Are you that hungry?" Carole asked.

"No," Stevie said. "I just don't want to be late."

"Okay, okay," said Carole. She gave Starlight a final pat. "Bye, fella. I'll see you a little later."

The two girls walked out of the cool darkness of the stable into the summer brightness. "It's really hot today," Stevie complained as they walked across the parking lot. "Why don't we go to my house and take a swim after TD's?"

"I thought we were coming back to the stable for a ride," Carole said.

"Oh, yeah," Stevie replied. She shrugged. "Guess I forgot."

They walked the short distance to TD's, arriving there only five minutes late. Lisa was waiting for them in their regular booth. "Hi, guys!" she called when they walked in the door.

"Hi!" Carole said, scooting into the booth beside her. "Did you get Jamie home okay?"

Lisa nodded. "He told his mother he had a great time and asked her if he could start taking some real riding lessons."

"What did she say?" asked Stevie.

"She said she thought that was a good idea, and she asked me for Max's number."

"All right!" Carole held up her hands for a high fifteen. "Another rider for Pine Hollow, and another convert for The Saddle Club!"

"And he'll make a good rider, too," Lisa said thoughtfully. "He's not afraid of horses, and he's gentle with the reins."

"Maybe he'll go to the Olympics and be a big star," Carole predicted. "Then we can say we're the ones who put him on his first horse."

"And nearly killed him with kindness at the Cross County Fair," added Stevie.

The girls were wondering what type of riding Jamie might go into when the waitress arrived at their table, order pad in hand.

"Let me guess," she said. She pointed her pencil at Lisa and Carole. "You two will have your usuals—a dish of chocolate with marshmallow sauce and a double cone of strawberry and pistachio, right?"

"Right," Lisa and Carole answered together.

The waitress scribbled on her pad, turned to a clean page,

then looked at Stevie. "Now," she said wearily. "You. What new frontiers of ice cream cuisine are we striving for today?"

Stevie looked at her friends and sighed. "I'd like a dish of vanilla, please."

For a moment no one spoke. In fact, for a moment no one even moved. Everyone was too shocked to do anything.

"And?" the waitress finally managed to say.

"And nothing," replied Stevie. "Just a dish of vanilla ice cream."

The waitress stared at Steve, her mouth agape. "What? No nuts? No pineapple sauce with peppermint chunks? No chocolate sprinkles with pretzel *garni*?"

"No thank you." Stevie shrugged. "Just vanilla."

The waitress squinted at Stevie for a long moment, then turned back toward the counter. "Kids," she mumbled, shaking her head. "Go figure."

Lisa put her hand on Stevie's forehead as soon as the waitress left. Carole grabbed her wrist to take her pulse.

"What are you doing?" Stevie cried irritably. "All I did was ask for vanilla ice cream."

"We know," replied Lisa. "That's what's so scary!"

Carole pressed her fingers into Stevie's wrist. "Well," she finally announced. "From all I can tell, she's still got a pulse."

"I'm telling you, I'm fine!" Stevie insisted. "I just felt like vanilla today."

"Listen, Stevie. If Carole and I have learned anything about misdiagnosing problems in the past two weeks, it's that when someone goes from ordering three different flavors of

132

ice cream with three different sauces to just plain vanilla, something's wrong. And we're going to get to the bottom of it."

"But I just feel like—"

"Wait a minute, Stevie." Carole frowned. "When did you say you had chicken pox?"

"When I was little. The same time Alex had them."

"But you don't really remember anything about them, do you?" Lisa said.

"No, I don't. I was too little," Stevie said.

"Right. But you remember Alex having chicken pox, and Alex having to take an oatmeal bath, don't you? If you'd had chicken pox, don't you think you'd remember at least some little something about it?"

"Well, no, I don't know . . ."

Carole looked at Lisa, then turned to Stevie. "Stevie, unbutton your shirt."

"Right here? In public?" Stevie answered in a goofy high voice, and batted her eyelashes extravagantly. "Please!"

"Stevie!" Carole warned.

"Okay, okay." Stevie unbuttoned her collar and peered down into the darkness inside her shirt. "Can't see a thing," she announced happily. "Looks like the misdiagnosis twins have struck again!"

"Wanna bet?" Carole got up, walked around the table, and pulled Stevie's shirttail up from her pants. She and Lisa gasped. A fine rash of tiny red dots speckled Stevie's stomach.

"It's chicken pox!" Carole and Lisa cried at the same time.

For once Stevie was stunned into silence. She sat there with her mouth open, staring at her stomach.

"We've got to get you home," Carole said. "Lisa, go cancel our ice cream."

"Okay." Lisa got up and ran to the counter.

"I don't know what to say," Stevie began.

"Don't say anything, Stevie. Chicken pox happens to the best of us." Carole reached down in her backpack for the small plastic bag Jamie had given her earlier that morning and held it out to her. "Take this home with you. Pegasus helped remind Jamie when he was sick that he would soon be riding Nickel again. Now Pegasus can do the same for you."

"But what if it's not chicken pox?" asked Stevie.

"If it's not chicken pox, then it must be lice or botflies," Lisa said as she returned to the table. "In that case, Dr. Hanson and I will give you a good grooming, shave your hair, burn all your clothes, and apply insecticide."

Carole laughed, still holding Pegasus out to Stevie. "Yeah, Stevie. You can take your choice. It's either the horseflies or the flying horse."

Stevie put the bundled-up Pegasus into her shirt pocket and looked at Carole and Lisa. "Since you put it that way," she said with a tired smile, "I'll take the flying horse and friends like you any day!"

What happens to The Saddle Club next?
Read Bonnie Bryant's exciting new series
and find out.

High school. Driver's licenses. Boyfriends. Jobs.

A lot of new things are happening, but one thing remains the same: Stevie Lake, Lisa Atwood, and Carole Hanson are still best friends. However, even among best friends some things do change, and problems can strain any friendship . . . but these three can handle it. Can't they?

Read an excerpt from Pine Hollow #1: *The Long Ride*.

PROLOGUE

"Do you think we'll get there in time?" Stevie Lake asked, looking around for some reassuring sign that the airport was near.

"Since that plane almost landed on us, I think it's safe to say that we're close," Carole Hanson said.

"Turn right here," said Callie Forester from the backseat.

"And then left up ahead," Carole advised, picking out directions from the signs that flashed past near the airport entrance. "I think Lisa's plane is leaving from that terminal there."

"Which one?"

"The one we just passed," Callie said.

"Oh," said Stevie. She gripped the steering wheel tightly and looked for a way to turn around without causing a major traffic tie-up.

"This would be easier if we were on horseback," said Carole.

"Everything's easier on horseback," Stevie agreed.

"Or if we had a police escort," said Callie.

"Have you done that?" Stevie asked, trying to maneuver the car across three lanes of traffic.

"I have," said Callie. "It's kind of fun, but dangerous. It makes you think you're almost as important as other people tell you you are."

Stevie rolled her window down and waved wildly at the confused drivers around her. Clearly, her waving confused them more, but it worked. All traffic stopped. She crossed the necessary three lanes and pulled onto the service road.

It took another ten minutes to get back to the right and then ten more to find a parking place. Five minutes into the terminal. And then all that was left was to find Lisa.

"Where do you think she is?" Carole asked.

"I know," said Stevie. "Follow me."

"That's what we've been doing all morning," Callie said dryly. "And look how far it's gotten us."

But she followed anyway.

ALEX LAKE REACHED across the table in the airport cafeteria and took Lisa Atwood's hand.

"It's going to be a long summer," he said.

Lisa nodded. Saying good-bye was one of her least favorite activities. She didn't want Alex to know how hard it was, though. That would just make it tougher on him. The two of them had known each other for four years—as long as Lisa had been best friends with Alex's twin sister, Stevie. But they'd only started dating six months earlier. Lisa could hardly believe that. It seemed as if she'd been in love with him forever.

"But it' is just for the summer," she said. The words sounded dumb even as they came out of her mouth. The summer *was* long. She wouldn't come back to Virginia until right before school started.

"I wish your dad didn't live so far away, and I wish the summer weren't so long."

"It'll go fast," said Lisa.

"For you, maybe. You'll be in California, surfing or something. I'll just be here, mowing lawns."

"I've never surfed in my life—"

"Until now," said Alex. It was almost a challenge, and Lisa didn't like it.

"I don't want to fight with you," said Lisa.

"I don't want to fight with you, either," he said, relenting. "I'm sorry. It's just that I want things to be different. Not very different. Just a little different."

"Me too," said Lisa. She squeezed his hand. It was a way to keep from saying anything else, because she was afraid that if she tried to speak she might cry, and she hated it when she cried. It made her face red and puffy, but most of all, it told other people how she was feeling. She'd found it useful to keep her feelings to herself these days. Like Alex, she wanted things to be different, but she wanted them to be very different, not just a little. She sighed. That was slightly better than crying.

"I TOLD YOU SO," said Stevie to Callie and Carole.

Stevie had threaded her way through the airport terminal, straight to the cafeteria near the security checkpoint. And there, sitting next to the door, were her twin brother and her best friend.

"Surprise!" the three girls cried, crowding around the table.

"We just couldn't let you be the only one to say goodbye to Lisa," Carole said, sliding into the booth next to Alex.

"We had to be here, too. You understand that, don't you?" Stevie asked Lisa as she sat down next to her.

"And since I was in the car, they brought me along," said Callie, pulling up a chair from a nearby table.

"You guys!" said Lisa, her face lighting up with joy. "I'm so glad you're here. I was afraid I wasn't going to see you for months and months!"

She *was* glad they were there. It wouldn't have felt right if she'd had to leave without seeing them one more time. "I thought you had other things to do."

"We just told you that so we could surprise you. We did surprise you, didn't we?"

"You surprised me," Lisa said, beaming.

"Me too," Alex said dryly. "I'm surprised, too. I really thought I could go for an afternoon, just *one* afternoon of my life, without seeing my twin sister."

Stevie grinned. "Well, there's always tomorrow," she said. "And that's something to look forward to, right?"

"Right," he said, grinning back.

Since she was closest to the outside, Callie went and got sodas for herself, Stevie, and Carole. When she rejoined the group, they were talking about everything in the world except the fact that Lisa was going to be gone for the summer and how much they were all going to miss one another.

She passed the drinks around and sat quietly at the end of the table. There wasn't much for her to say. She didn't really feel as if she belonged there. She wasn't anybody's best friend. It wasn't as if they minded her being there, but she'd come along because Stevie had offered to drive her to a tack shop after they left the airport. She was simply along for the ride.

". . . And don't forget to say hello to Skye."

"Skye? Skye who?" asked Alex.

"Don't pay any attention to him," Lisa said. "He's just jealous."

"You mean because Skye is a movie star?"

"And say hi to your father and the new baby. It must be exciting that you'll meet your sister."

"Well, of course, you've already met her, but now she's crawling, right? It's a whole different thing."

An announcement over the PA system brought their chatter to a sudden halt.

"It's my flight," Lisa said slowly. "They're starting to board and I've got to get through security and then to Gate . . . whatever."

"Fourteen," Alex said. "It comes after Gate Twelve. There are no thirteens in airports."

"Let's go."

"Here, I'll carry that."

"And I'll get this one . . ."

As Callie watched, Lisa hugged Carole and Stevie. Then she kissed Alex. Then she hugged her friends again. Then she turned to Alex.

"I think it's time for us to go," Carole said tactfully.

"Write or call every day," Stevie said.

"It's a promise," said Lisa. "Thanks for coming to the airport. You, too, Callie."

Callie smiled and gave Lisa a quick hug before all the girls backed off from Lisa and Alex.

Lisa waved. Her friends waved and turned to leave her alone with Alex. They were all going to miss her, but the girls had one another. Alex only had his lawns to mow. He needed the last minutes with Lisa.

"See you at home!" Stevie called over her shoulder, but she didn't think Alex heard. His attention was completely focused on one person.

Carole wiped a tear from her eye once they'd rounded a corner. "I'm going to miss her."

"Me too," said Stevie.

Carole turned to Callie. "It must be hard for you to understand," she said.

"Not really," said Callie. "I can tell you three are really close."

"We are," Carole said. "Best friends for a long time. We're practically inseparable." Even to her the words sounded exclusive and uninviting. If Callie noticed, she didn't say anything.

The three girls walked out of the terminal and found their way to Stevie's car. As she turned on the engine, Stevie was aware of an uncomfortable empty feeling. She really didn't like the idea of Lisa's being gone for the summer, and her own unhappiness was not going to be helped by a brother who was going to spend the entire time moping about his missing girlfriend. There had to be something that would make her feel better.

"Say, Carole, do you want to come along with us to the tack shop?" she asked.

"No, I can't," Carole said. "I promised I'd bring in the horses from the paddock before dark, so you can just drop me off at Pine Hollow. Anyway, aren't you due at work in an hour?"

Stevie glanced at her watch. Carole was right. Everything was taking longer than it was supposed to this afternoon.

"Don't worry," Callie said quickly. "We can go to the tack shop another time."

"You don't mind?" Stevie asked.

"No. I don't. Really," said Callie. "I don't want you to be late for work—either of you. If my parents decide to get a pizza for dinner again, I'm going to want it to arrive on time!"

Stevie laughed, but not because she thought anything was very funny. She wasn't about to forget the last time she'd delivered a pizza to Callie's family. In fact, she wished it hadn't happened, but it had. Now she had to find a way to face up to it.

As she pulled out of the airport parking lot, a plane roared overhead, rising into the brooding sky. *Maybe that's Lisa's plane*, she thought. The noise of its flight seemed to mark the beginning of a long summer.

The first splats of rain hit the windshield as Stevie paid their way out of the parking lot. By the time they were on the highway, it was raining hard. The sky had darkened to a steely gray. Streaks of lightning brightened it, only to be followed by thunder that made the girls jump.

The storm had come out of nowhere. Stevie flicked on the windshield wipers and hoped it would go right back to nowhere.

The sky turned almost black as the storm strengthened. Curtains of rain ripped across the windshield, pounding on the hood and roof of the car. The wipers flicked uselessly at the torrent.

"I hope Fez is okay," said Callie. "He hates thunder, you know."

"I'm not surprised," said Carole, trying to control her voice. It seemed to her that there were a lot of things Fez hated. He was as temperamental as any horse she had ever ridden.

Fez was one of the horses in the paddock. Carole didn't want to upset Callie by telling her that. If she told Callie he'd been turned out, Callie would wonder why he hadn't just been exercised. If she told Callie she'd exercised him, Callie might wonder if he was being overworked. Carole shook her head. What was it about this girl that made Carole so certain that whatever she said, it would be wrong? Why couldn't she say the one thing she really needed to say?

Still, Carole worked at Pine Hollow, and that meant taking care of the horses that were boarding there—and that meant keeping the owners happy.

"I'm sure Fez will be fine. Ben and Max will look after him," Carole said.

"I guess you're right," said Callie. "I know he can be difficult. Of course, you've ridden him, so you know that, too. I mean, that's obvious. But it's spirit, you see. Spirit is the key to an endurance specialist. He's got it, and I think he's got the makings of a champion. We'll work together this summer, and come fall . . . well, you'll see."

Spirit—yes, it was important in a horse. Carole knew that. She just wished she understood why it was that Fez's spirit was so irritating to her. She'd always thought of herself as someone who'd never met a horse she didn't like. Maybe it was the horse's owner . . .

"Uh-oh," said Stevie, putting her foot gently on the brake. "I think I got it going a little too fast there."

"You've got to watch out for that," Callie said. "My father says the police practically lie in wait for teenage drivers. They love to give us tickets. Well, they certainly had fun with me."

"You got a ticket?" Stevie asked.

"No, I just got a warning, but it was almost worse than a ticket. I was going four miles over the speed limit in our hometown. The policeman stopped me, and when he saw who I was, he just gave me a warning. Dad was furious—at me and at the officer, though he didn't say anything to the officer. He was angry at him because he thought someone would find out and say I'd gotten special treatment! I was only going four miles over the speed limit. Really. Even the officer said that. Well, it would have been easier if I'd gotten a ticket. Instead, I got grounded. Dad won't let me drive for three months. Of course, that's nothing compared to what happened to Scott last year."

"What happened to Scott?" Carole asked, suddenly curious about the driving challenges of the Forester children.

"Well, it's kind of a long story," said Callie. "But—"

"Wow! Look at that!" Stevie interrupted. There was an amazing streak of lightning over the road ahead. The dark afternoon brightened for a minute. Thunder followed instantly.

"Maybe we should pull off the road or something?" Carole suggested.

"I don't think so," said Stevie. She squinted through the windshield. "It's not going to last long. It never does when it rains this hard. We get off at the next exit anyway."

She slowed down some more and turned the wipers up a notch. She followed the car in front of her, keeping a constant eye on the two red spots of the car's taillights. She'd be okay as long as she could see them. The rain pelted the car so loudly that it was hard to talk. Stevie drove on cautiously.

Then, as suddenly as it had started, the rain stopped. Stevie spotted the sign for their exit, signaled, and pulled off to the right and up the ramp. She took a left onto the overpass and followed the road toward Willow Creek.

The sky was as dark as it had been, and there were clues that there had been some rain there, but nothing nearly as hard as the rain they'd left on the interstate. Stevie sighed with relief and switched the windshield wipers to a slower rate.

"I think I'll drop you off at Pine Hollow first," she said, turning onto the road that bordered the stable's property.

Pine Hollow's white fences followed the contour of the road, breaking the open, grassy hillside into a sequence of paddocks and fields. A few horses stood in the fields, swishing their tails. One bucked playfully and ran up a hill, shaking his head to free his mane in the wind. Stevie smiled. Horses always seemed to her the most welcoming sight in the world.

"Then I'll take Callie home," Stevie continued, "and after that I'll go over to Pizza Manor. I may be a few minutes late for work, but who orders pizza at five o'clock in the afternoon anyway?"

"Now, now," teased Carole. "Is that any way for you to mind your Pizza Manors?"

"Well, at least I have my hat with me," said Stevie. Or did she? She looked into the rearview mirror to see if she could spot it, and when that didn't do any good, she glanced over her shoulder. Callie picked it up and started to hand it to her.

"Here," she said. "We wouldn't want— Wow! I guess the storm isn't over yet!"

The sky had suddenly filled with a brilliant streak of lightning, jagged and pulsating, accompanied by an explosion of thunder.

It startled Stevie. She shrieked and turned her face back to the road. The light was so sudden and so bright that it blinded her for a second. The car swerved. Stevie braked. She clutched at the steering wheel and then realized she couldn't see because the rain was pelting even harder than before. She reached for the wiper control, switching it to its fastest speed.

There was something to her right! She saw something move, but she didn't know what it was.

"Stevie!" Carole cried.

"Look out!" Callie screamed from the backseat.

Stevie swerved to the left on the narrow road, hoping it would be enough. Her answer was a sickening jolt as the car slammed into something solid. The car spun around, smashing against the thing again. When the thing screamed, Stevie knew it was a horse. Then it disappeared from her field of vision. Once again, the car spun. It smashed against the guardrail on the left side of the road and tumbled up and over it as if the rail had never been there.

Down they went, rolling, spinning. Stevie could hear the screams of her friends. She could hear her own voice, echoing in the close confines of the car, answered by the thumps of the car rolling down the hillside into a gully. Suddenly the thumping stopped. The screams were stilled. The engine cut off. The wheels stopped spinning. And all Stevie could hear was the idle *slap, slap slap* of her windshield wipers.

"Carole?" she whispered. "Are you okay?"

"I think so. What about you?" Carole answered.

"Me too. Callie? Are you okay?" Stevie asked.

There was no answer.

"Callie?" Carole echoed.

The only response was the girl's shallow breathing.

How could this have happened?

ABOUT THE AUTHOR

Bonnie Bryant is the author of nearly a hundred books about horses, including The Saddle Club series, Saddle Club Super Editions, and the Pony Tails series. She has also written novels and movie novelizations under her married name, B. B. Hiller.

Ms. Bryant began writing The Saddle Club in 1986. Although she had done some riding before that, she intensified her studies then and found herself learning right along with her characters Stevie, Carole, and Lisa. She claims that they are all much better riders than she is.

Ms. Bryant was born and raised in New York City. She still lives there, in Greenwich Village, with her two sons.

Don't miss Bonnie Bryant's next exciting
Saddle Club Adventures . . .

ENGLISH HORSE
The Saddle Club #79

The Saddle Club girls are getting ready for the arrival of
their friend Lady Theresa, otherwise known as Tessa,
from England. She's going to be spending time in Willow Creek, and they can't wait. To The Saddle Club,
Tessa's visit means fun, sleepovers, and, of course,
horses! To Veronica diAngelo, however, Tessa's arrival
means a chance for revenge. Veronica has never forgotten how this cousin of the Queen snubbed her when
they were in England—and now it's Veronica's turn.

Will Veronica start a new revolutionary war? Or can
The Saddle Club keep the peace?

And read the companion to this book, *English Rider*.

ENGLISH RIDER
The Saddle Club #80

Tessa and Veronica best friends? That's the way it looks. Instead of hanging out with The Saddle Club, their visiting English friend Lady Theresa is spending all her time with Veronica diAngelo. They talk together, shop together, and even ride together! Veronica is thrilled and can already see herself being invited back to England to meet Tessa's cousins—namely, the royal family. Stevie, Carole, and Lisa are confused. They thought Veronica hated Tessa since Tessa snubbed her back in England. Have they lost one of their best friends to their worst enemy?

Could it be that Veronica and Tessa have managed to bury the hatchet? Or is something else going on?